CW00820462

Unexplored

Anna Hackett

Unexplored

Published by Anna Hackett
Copyright 2016 by Anna Hackett
Cover by Melody Simmons of eBookindiecovers
Edits by Tanya Saari

ISBN (eBook): 978-0-9945572-8-5
ISBN (paperback): 978-1-925539-02-8

This book is a work of fiction. All names, characters, places and incidents are either the product of the author's imagination or are used fictitiously. Any resemblance to actual persons, events or places is coincidental. No part of this book may be reproduced, scanned, or distributed in any printed or electronic form.

What readers are saying about Anna's Romances

At Star's End – One of Library Journal's Best E-Original Romances for 2014

Return to Dark Earth – One of Library Journal's Best E-Original Books for 2015 and two-time SFR Galaxy Awards winner

The Phoenix Adventures – SFR Galaxy Award Winner for Most Fun New Series and "Why Isn't This a Movie?" Series

Beneath a Trojan Moon – SFR Galaxy Award Winner and RWAus Ella Award Winner

Hell Squad – Amazon Bestselling Sci-fi Romance Series and SFR Galaxy Award Winner

"Like Indiana Jones meets Star Wars. A treasure hunt with a steamy romance." – SFF Dragon, review of *Among Galactic Ruins*

"Fun, action-packed read that I thoroughly enjoyed. The romance was steamy, there's a whole heap of supporting characters I can't wait to get to know better and there's enough archeology and history to satisfy my inner geek." – Book Gannet Reviews review of *Undiscovered*

"Strap in, enjoy the heat of romance and the daring of this group of space travellers!" – Di, Top 500 Amazon Reviewer, review of *At Star's End*

Don't miss out! For updates about new releases, action romance info, free books, and other fun stuff, sign up for my VIP mailing list and get your *free box set* containing three action-packed romances.

Visit here to get started:

www.annahackettbooks.com

Chapter One

Thank God her crappy day was almost over.

Sydney Granger walked into her office, wanting nothing more than to kick off her high heels. Her aching feet were killing her. She sighed. But she still had work to do before she could head back to her condo and relax with a glass of wine.

She sank down in the black-leather office chair behind her sleek, glossy desk. The meeting with the board had…not gone well. She touched her aching temple. It had been two months since she'd taken over as CEO of Granger Industries, and the board members were still nervous. All they saw was a wealthy heiress who was inexperienced in business, real estate, and construction.

Sydney shrugged to herself. She was used to people underestimating her.

She swiveled in her chair and, for a second, stared out at the glowing lights of Washington, D.C. She had an excellent view of the grand dome of the Capitol Building. She knew D.C.—had been born and raised here—but she was still finding her feet in the new job. And behind closed doors, she secretly wondered if she'd ever get there.

Glancing back at her desk, she saw the files stacked neatly on the corner by her executive assistant. Then she looked at her laptop. Sydney knew if she opened it, she'd have a ton of emails to deal with. That glass of wine had never seemed further away.

What the hell...there was no one left in the office at this time of night, so she released the clip in her hair. No one to see the new CEO kicking back. The pale-gold strands fell down to brush her shoulders.

Her gaze fell on the framed photo resting on the corner of her desk. It was a picture of her with her father and brother. It had been taken a few years ago, and they were all grinning for the camera. *Why the hell did you leave me the company, Dad?* Still reeling from her father's sudden death, she'd been stunned when he'd left the lion's share of the company to her. Her brother, Drew, had inherited stock in the company as well. Drew had a sky-high IQ, and probably knew way more about the business and the company. But she knew that for all his brilliance, her socially awkward brother wasn't a businessman.

For some reason, her father had wanted *her* to be CEO of Granger.

God, she missed him. Since her mother had died when Sydney was ten, it had just been the three of them. Grief and guilt were a gnawing hollow ache inside her. But Sydney didn't let it show. She'd been raised in Washington society, and she was damn good at hiding her feelings. At the glittering gatherings, so many people were just waiting for the slightest show of emotion to pounce and spread the gossip. She remembered the insincere faces and condescending pats after her mother had died.

Sydney leaned back in her chair. The CIA should just send their agents to train at society parties and gallery openings. Then they'd have the best poker faces around. She touched the frame. Had it really been two months since her father had died in that explosion? Terrorists had been targeting a foreign diplomat who'd been staying at the same hotel, and her father had been caught in the blast.

"I'm so sorry, Dad."

Now, Sydney was here, buried in her work at Granger Industries. Drew, unable to cope, had run off to South America. His latest interest was in history and archeology. The guy had a collection of degrees—she sighed—but he never stuck with one thing. Last month, he'd been talking about launching an online tech company. Next month, who knew? He'd probably take up race car driving.

Sydney rubbed her temple again. She had reports to read, forms to sign, tomorrow's meetings to prepare for. She was trying, but right now, she just felt like she was drowning. Most days she was barely managing to keep her head above water.

It had to get better, but there was a little voice in the back of her head whispering with a whole lot of glee that she'd fail. Again. It loved to remind her that she'd screwed up her last job…and that others had paid the price. She glanced over at the photo of her father again, and her throat tightened.

The ringing of the phone on her desk startled

her. She frowned. It was late. Who'd be calling at this time?

She snatched up the receiver. "Sydney Granger."

"Ms. Granger, listen and do not talk."

The electronically-altered voice made her stiffen. "Who is this—?"

"Quiet. Your brother's life depends on it."

Sydney's hand clenched on the phone. "This is about Drew?"

"We have your brother in Peru. If you want him back alive, you come to Lima and be prepared to transfer five million dollars to us to secure his freedom. We will contact you again then."

What? Her heart started to pound. *Stay calm, Sydney. Keep them talking. Get as much information as you can.* "How do I know this isn't a hoax?" She looked blindly out the window, the lights of the city now just a blur. "I want to talk with him—"

"I make the demands, not you. My only proof...I am Silk Road."

The line went dead.

Sydney set the phone back down with a shaky hand. Silk Road? Who the hell was Silk Road?

She'd spoken to Drew a few days ago. He'd been fine. Excited. He was on the trail of an ancient pre-Incan culture. He'd been visiting museums, meeting with local archeologists, and talking about heading into the Andes. He'd been yammering on about the ruins he planned to visit, and talking about all the research he'd been doing.

But for all his amazing intelligence, her brother

was a bit oblivious to regular life. It would be so easy to snatch him.

God. If these people hurt him... Drew was all Sydney had left.

She forced herself to breathe. *Think, Sydney.* Did this have something to do with her previous employment? Her former role had been highly classified. None of her friends or family had known about the work she'd done. To the world, she'd been a Washington socialite who cared mostly about designer clothes, fancy parties, and museum openings.

She quickly opened her laptop and logged on. She typed in a search on Silk Road.

A few minutes later, she sat back in her chair, dread settling in her belly. There wasn't much, but what she'd learned wasn't good. Silk Road appeared to be a dangerous, black-market antiquities syndicate. Not much was known about them, except that they were well-funded, well-connected, and ruthless.

Something else caught her attention. Over the last few months, the group had tangled with a private security firm that specialized in security for archeological digs, expeditions, and museum exhibits. Treasure Hunter Security. She tilted her head at the fun name. It appeared that this firm had beaten Silk Road—twice.

She typed in another search, and pulled up the website for Treasure Hunter Security.

They were based in Denver but worked all across the world. She scrolled through the pages and stopped at an image showing three men—all of them wearing khaki clothes and holsters—standing shoulder-to-shoulder. Declan and Callum Ward were the owners of the company. Former Navy SEALs, and from the look of them, tough and capable. Her gaze fell on the third man standing with them. He was slightly taller and a little broader than the Ward brothers. Big, with shaggy, long, brown hair and a rugged face. He looked like a man you didn't want to mess with.

Her gaze drifted back to the photograph on her desk and locked onto her brother's smiling face. Her stomach turned over.

She had to rescue Drew. And she needed Treasure Hunter Security to help her do it.

***

Logan O'Connor stretched out, put his boots up on the arm of the couch and pulled his ball cap over his eyes.

Damn, he was tired.

After he'd returned from a job in the Cambodian jungle a month back—having rescued Callum's ass—he'd plunged straight into another job in the Gobi Desert. It'd been grueling, and hot, and sandy. He hated sand.

"Hey, boots off the couch!" A hand slapped at his boots.

Logan just growled.

His hat was whipped away. Darcy Ward stood there, glaring at him. As usual, she was all glossy and put-together. Not a single strand of her chin-length black hair was out of place and her blue-gray eyes were narrowed on him.

She tried to shift his boots again, but he kept them where they were.

"We have a client coming in, Logan," she said with a huff.

Logan grunted.

She pushed and shoved again, and finally his feet slid off to the polished concrete floor.

He sat up. "I'm damn glad I never had a sister."

She pulled a face at him.

"Go bother your *actual* brothers," he growled.

"They aren't here." Her nose screwed up. "Declan and Layne are upstairs. They should be down soon."

Dec—Logan's best friend—lived in the apartment above the Treasure Hunter Security offices.

Logan snorted. "I bet I know what the hell they're doing." Since his best friend had tumbled head-over-his-ass in love with Dr. Layne Rush, the man couldn't seem to stay away from his fiancée. "Those two are like fucking rabbits."

"No swearing in the office," Darcy snapped.

"Why?"

"We have a client coming in," she said with exaggerated patience. "She's flying in from D.C. She's the CEO of Granger Industries. This is going to be a good-paying job, Logan. Don't screw anything up."

Granger Industries? Logan had a vague

recollection of real estate, or construction, or something. Just to piss Darcy off, Logan put his boots up on the coffee table. "Where's Cal?"

"On a trip with Dani. She's photographing the ruined city of Great Zimbabwe and Cal went with her."

Another man who couldn't stay away from his woman. Logan still couldn't believe his friends had gone and fallen in love. Dec and Cal—two of the toughest guys he'd ever known.

He heard footsteps, and since he hadn't heard the front door, he knew it was Dec. Actually, after years together on the SEAL teams, and now working together at THS, Logan could pick out Dec's footsteps anywhere.

"Darce. Logan." Declan crossed the large, open space of the converted warehouse.

Logan glanced at his friend. Dec was tall, muscled, with piercing gray eyes. He still looked the same as he always had, but these days, he seemed different. More relaxed, more at ease.

"Who's our new client?" Dec asked.

"Sydney Granger of Granger Industries." Darcy looked at her watch. "Her plane should've landed about an hour ago. She should be here soon."

Dec nodded and headed toward the small kitchenette in the corner of the space. He opened the fridge and pulled out a soda.

"Diet Coke?" Logan raised a brow.

"Layne is addicted to the stuff." Dec shrugged. "I've developed a taste for it."

Logan shook his head. "Next thing you'll tell me

is that you want to do lunch, or go out for a damned manicure."

Dec's gray gaze narrowed. "No, but I'm thinking about kicking your ass."

Logan snorted. "You can try."

"Shush," Darcy said. "She's here. Try to look professional." She knocked Logan's boots off the coffee table.

Logan followed Darcy's gaze to the wall of flat screens at the end of the warehouse. That was Darcy's domain. She might look like she'd stepped out of a magazine, but the woman was a genius with computers. On the far screen, he saw security footage from the outside of the office. He saw what looked like a rental car parked near his truck, and caught a glimpse of blonde hair as a woman walked toward the front door of the warehouse.

The next thing he heard was the click of heels on concrete. Logan turned his head. And then he straightened.

The woman was tall, slender, and wearing a navy blue skirt that slicked over her gentle curves and a crisp white shirt. Blonde hair the color of champagne was caught back in some sort of complicated twist at the back of her head, accenting a face that was downright beautiful. She had a slim nose, perfectly formed lips, and high cheekbones. Pale-blue eyes skated over the room.

The woman had money and class written all over her.

Logan shifted on the couch. She was *so* not his type.

"Hi, Ms. Granger." Darcy stepped forward and held out her hand. "I'm Darcy Ward. This is my brother Declan."

"Thank you for seeing me. And please, call me Sydney." She shook hands with Darcy and then with Declan.

"Nice to meet you," Dec said.

"And this is one of our top security specialists, Logan O'Connor." Darcy gestured at Logan.

Logan didn't bother standing, just lifted his chin.

Sydney Granger gave him a cool stare before her gaze moved back to Declan and Darcy.

Yeah, he'd been dismissed by the Ice Queen. He was surprised he didn't have freezer burn.

"I need your help," Sydney said. "My brother needs your help."

Darcy gestured to the conference table off to the side. "Why don't you sit down? You wouldn't give us any details over the phone—"

Sydney Granger nodded. "I wasn't sure if it was safe." She sank into a chair. "My brother left for Peru several weeks ago. He has a history degree, and he wanted to explore an ancient culture down there—"

"Inca?" Dec asked.

"No. Have you ever heard of the Warriors of the Clouds? They're also called the Chachapoyas."

Logan frowned, and watched Darcy and Dec shake their heads. Darcy reached over to tap on one of her keyboards, clearly planning to do a search.

"I hadn't either," Sydney answered. "But I did

some research on the flight out here."

"They're from *Raiders of the Lost Ark*," Logan said.

Pretty blue eyes blinked at him. "Yes."

Yeah, I'm not just a big, dumb idiot. Logan was used to people taking one look at him and deciding he was big and dangerous but not very smart.

"The gold idol that Indy's after in the beginning of the movie—" he looked at the others "—you know, when he's escaping from the big, rolling boulder. That belonged to these warriors."

"That's right," Sydney Granger said in her cool, cultured voice. "But the movie isn't factual. The Chachapoyas weren't metalworkers, so they didn't have any golden idols. But they built cities and fortresses high in the cloud forests of the Andes. My brother estimated that only a small portion of their sites have been found so far. The Cloud Warriors fought off the Inca for years, and even helped the Spanish fight against the Inca. They were famed for being beautiful, and many of them were fair-skinned with pale-colored hair and eyes. Several of their mummies have been discovered, and some do have pale hair, and several descendants of the Chachapoyas today still have blonde hair, and blue or green eyes."

"Were they not native to the region?" Darcy asked. "Perhaps they came from somewhere else?"

Sydney tilted her head. "There are lots of theories. That they had come from Europe prior to the Spanish, that they were descended from the white, bearded god, Viracocha. Recent DNA testing shows they are from the Andes, indistinguishable from the others living in the area. They are from the cloud forests."

"What happened to the Cloud Warriors?" Logan asked.

"They held out, but eventually the Inca conquered them. They were forced to leave their cities, and then disease brought by the Spanish wiped them out."

"Okay, so what do these Warriors of the Clouds have to do with your brother?" Dec asked.

Logan watched the woman as she lifted her chin. Staring at her face, all he saw was icy perfection. No emotion, no distress, nothing. Yeah, she was a real cool one.

"I got a call at my office last night. A group says it has my brother and they want five million dollars in ransom. They said I have to go to Lima, Peru to carry out the transaction."

Logan shook his head to himself. Forget cool, she was ice all the way. Man, the woman didn't even look like her pulse jumped when she talked about her brother being held hostage. Ice water in those veins.

Dec was frowning. "We don't do a lot of ransom demands. We have interceded when some archeologists have been snatched off digs—"

Interestingly, Logan saw Sydney press her hands together on the table. Her fingers flexed, then relaxed. "I came to you because the group who have Drew...they call themselves Silk Road."

Now, Logan pushed to his feet. *Aw, hell.*

Chapter Two"I know you've had some experience with Silk Road," Sydney said, desperately controlling the emotions rolling inside her. "That's why I came to you."

"You could say that." Declan Ward exchanged a glance with the big bear of a man named Logan. "They're a black-market antiquities ring. They have money and no conscience."

His words made Sydney's skin go cold. And these people had Drew. "Will you help me? My brother is the only family I have left." Grief and fear melded together inside her, and she fought back a shiver. Suddenly, she was very cold. She dug her nails into her palms to keep from letting any of it show on her face.

She saw Declan share another look with the intimidating Logan.

Darcy stood. "Why don't you let me run some searches? Let me see if we can find out what's going on down in Lima."

"I've tried to contact the authorities—"

Darcy nodded. "It's difficult, I know. Distance, language barriers, different systems. Let me see what I can find." The brunette shot a look at Logan. "Logan, can you get Ms. Granger a drink?"

"A drink?" The big man looked confused. "I'm not a waiter."

Darcy rolled her eyes. "Well, I don't need you to shoot anybody for me right now, so get her a drink." Darcy strode over to the computers.

Sydney cleared her throat. "I'm fine—"

He made a noise, stomped over, and pulled out

her chair. "Come on. Kitchen's this way."

Seeing no way of politely getting out of it, she reluctantly followed him. Another shiver wracked her. The shock of everything that had happened was hitting her all at once. She rubbed her arms. She'd left her suit jacket in the car.

"What do you want to drink?"

The gruff, ungracious question came from the direction of the small, organized kitchenette tucked away in a corner of the large room.

"Water, please."

He snorted, and she watched as he grabbed a mug from a cupboard and a pot of coffee off a coffee maker.

"Didn't you hear me?" she asked.

"You're cold. You need something to warm up. Cream? Sugar?"

His overbearing tone made her bristle. "Black." She liked sugar in her coffee, but she'd be damned if she'd tell him that.

He shoved the mug at her. It was chipped on one edge and had World's Greatest Shot emblazoned on it.

"Sorry. This isn't high tea at the Ritz," he said.

Sydney bit back a smart retort and forced herself to calmly take a sip. As she did, she watched him start unbuttoning his shirt.

Her eyes widened, and she fought not to sputter her coffee everywhere. Underneath the well-worn blue shirt, he wore a gray T-shirt. It was stretched to breaking point across the large, hard planes of his chest. He shrugged his button-down shirt off, and then reached out and slipped it around her shoulders.

"What are you doing?" She hated that her voice sounded like a squeak.

"You're cold."

"I'm fine." Then the warmth from the fabric hit her. God, the man must run really hot. It felt so good on her chilled body. Her gaze moved over his muscled forearms and the gray fabric straining over his massive biceps. He shifted and she saw the backs of his arms were covered in tattoos. They looked like…the scratches of bear claws. He had claw marks tattooed on his arms. She quickly took another sip of coffee. She wasn't used to men like Logan O'Connor.

"You're not fine. You're shivering. You might have ice in your veins, but I won't let you freeze to death right in front of me."

She narrowed her gaze on him, hearing the contempt in his voice. "Ice in my veins?" She felt her temper spike. "I just got here. You don't know me."

"I know enough. Your brother's missing, and you're talking about it without a flicker of emotion. Like you couldn't care less. That's cold."

She took a deep breath. "You'd prefer to see me rant and scream and cry? Maybe I should throw in some hysterics for good measure?" Why was she even bothering with this man? He was a stranger. "Forget it. I don't have to deal with judgmental strangers who look like they just wandered out of the woods." She spun away from him.

With some relief, Sydney spotted Darcy waving them over.

"I can confirm that your brother was staying in Lima." Darcy's fingers flew over a keyboard. "He had a room at the Hotel San Antonio. No one has seen him there for the last twenty-four hours."

Sydney closed her eyes. *Oh, Drew.* She opened her eyes and saw that Logan was watching her.

"I'm running some searches now for any police reports," Darcy was saying. "Yes, I've got something. A few people reported an American man running down the street, being chased by a group of other men. That's all the details I have. We'll know more on the ground there."

"You'll help me?" Sydney's voice was a quiet whisper. She felt all the THS people watching her.

"Yes." Darcy reached out and pressed a hand to Sydney's arm. "My brothers and my adopted brothers—" she shot Logan a look "—drive me crazy most days, but I'd move heaven and earth to help if they were in trouble." A wry look crossed her face. "Actually, I've done it on numerous occasions."

Dec had a faint smile on his face. "Former Navy SEALs here. Usually we can rescue ourselves."

Darcy snorted. "It's a macho SEAL thing. They like to believe they're superheroes and don't need any help."

A small laugh escaped Sydney. She realized they were trying to cheer her up. Their easy camaraderie was nice…she loved Drew, but they didn't have a relationship like this. "So what happens now?"

"Logan and Declan will run this op. Along with two of our other specialists—Morgan Kincaid and Hale Carter."

Logan. Sydney tried not to show any reaction to that. When she lifted her gaze, it met the big man's startlingly golden eyes. His eyes made her think of her father's favorite Scotch. Or the eyes of a big, lazy lion ready to hunt.

Sydney schooled herself to show her most polite smile. "Wonderful."

"I'll call ahead to have our jet fueled and prepared," Declan said. "And I need to call Morgan and Hale. They'll meet us at the airport."

Logan nodded. "I'll need to stop by my place on the way. Get changed and grab my stuff."

Declan nodded. "I'll do the same and say goodbye to Layne. You can take Sydney with you, and I'll meet you guys at the airport."

Logan made a noise that reminded Sydney of a wild animal. An untamed beast.

After that, things moved fast. Sydney called out goodbye to Darcy, and found herself being ushered out of the warehouse. Logan led her over to a huge black truck with enormous tires. They stopped for a minute while he grabbed her bag out of the back of her rental car.

"Darce will make sure the rental gets returned." He lifted her Louis Vuitton suitcase and tossed it in the back of his truck.

Sydney opened the truck's passenger side door and eyed the height to get in. How the hell was she going to climb in with a pencil skirt on?

Suddenly, large hands circled her waist and she found herself boosted up onto the seat. Logan stared at her for a second, then stepped back and closed the door. Sydney sat there, pondering the fact that Logan O'Connor's hands could span her entire waist.

He climbed in behind the wheel and pulled his seatbelt on. "I don't live too far from here. We won't be long."

He drove them through downtown Denver, and then they headed east toward City Park. He drove with an easy confidence. Finally, he pulled up in front of a three-story, newish condo block and cut the engine.

"No cave?" The words just slipped out of Sydney's mouth.

His gaze narrowed on her, and for a second she imagined a flash of amusement. "You're coming in."

She felt her jaw tighten. "Do you not have any manners? You ask, O'Connor, not issue a gruff, rude order."

"I'm not one of your polite society guys. I don't really do fancy manners." He held up his large hands. "I don't have soft palms or wear fancy suits."

He said 'suits' like he was talking about a venomous animal. His hands were covered in nicks, scars, and calluses.

"Yes," she responded. "I can see that."

He got out, circled the truck, grabbed her bag, and yanked her door open. "You need to get changed as well. Unless you're planning to travel to

South America in your fancy designer clothes."

Sydney decided it would be more prudent just to go inside while he collected his things than continue the argument.

She followed him through a security gate and into an elevator. They walked across an open walkway and he paused to unlock a door. Then he ushered her into the condo, setting her bag down. She raised her brows. The place was clean, despite screaming *single guy*. While the kitchen was surprisingly well-decked-out, the rest of the place had a slightly sparse kind of feel to it. No pictures, no paint, no plants. She didn't figure Logan was one for home decorating.

"I'm going to take a quick shower and change." He waved at the black leather couch in front of an enormous flat-screen television. "Make yourself at home."

He walked through a door she guessed led to the master bedroom, and closed it behind him. Instead of sitting, Sydney wandered through the open-plan living room. On a mantle above the television, she spotted a couple of framed photos. One was a picture of him with a group of tough-looking guys wearing fatigues—what she guessed was his SEAL team. She spotted Logan—black paint spread over his face—his shoulder pressed up against Declan Ward's. The next photo showed a picture of a small boy with golden-brown eyes standing beside a hulk of a man in an Army uniform. She guessed Logan had come from a military family.

Tiredness and worry started to crowd in on her.

She sat on the edge of the couch and pulled out her cell phone. There was an image of Drew that she'd snapped when they'd had dinner just before he'd left for Peru. He'd been distant, and she'd known he was hurting from losing their father. She stroked the screen. She'd always felt protective of him. He'd finished school early and gone on to college. He didn't have the best social skills, could be clueless at times, but he was always smiling and friendly.

She hadn't wanted him to go to South America. But she'd been so busy taking over Granger, reeling from her guilt over her father, and, as Drew liked to remind her, he was an adult. She couldn't protect him from everything. Still, she should never have let him go to Peru. Tears pricked her eyes and she pressed her fist to her mouth to stifle her sob.

She heard a noise and looked up. Logan stood in the doorway with only a white towel wrapped around his lean hips.

Shock, and something else very hot that she refused to name, hit her system. He was hard and big. There was no fat on him and he had ropes of muscle across his chest. And his abs...she sucked in a breath. Those hard ridges of muscle didn't look real. His long, brown hair was damp and brushing his shoulders, framing that tough, rugged face.

Sydney's last lover had been a lawyer. And before him, she'd dated a workaholic lobbyist for a few months. She didn't recall any of them giving her this hard shock of heat just by looking at them. She'd never seen a man like Logan before. So big, so dominating, so primal.

"What's wrong?" His voice was a deep grumble.

"Nothing." She dashed her tears away, her other hand clenching on her phone.

"Did Silk Road contact you again?" He stalked over.

For a second, Sydney had the image of a wolf stalking its prey. He grabbed her hand and pried her fingers off the phone. Up this close, she smelled the scent of damp skin and soap. He glanced at the picture of her brother and then back at her face.

Then he scowled and pulled back. "I'll get dressed and then we'll get going. I suggest you change out of that skinny skirt and put on something more comfortable for traveling. Spare bathroom's that way." He jerked his head.

And just like that, he turned and stalked away. Now, she got a perfect view of his muscular back. It was covered in black ink, the lifelike image of a howling wolf.

Sydney released a shaky breath. She felt like she'd just barely survived a deadly encounter with something dangerous.

***

Logan stomped through Denver airport, his duffel bag slung over his shoulder, and holding Sydney's fancy suitcase in his hand. At least she'd changed back at his place. Now, instead of the fitted skirt, she wore dark denim jeans and a tailored jacket. Unfortunately, the jeans gave him a perfect view of long, slim legs and a perfectly shaped butt.

Dammit. Back at the warehouse, it had been easy to write her off as a high-society snob and unfeeling ice queen. But when he'd come out and seen her sitting on his couch, tears glittering in her eyes, he'd felt blindsided. He hadn't wanted to see beyond her cool exterior. He still hadn't decided if she was just controlled or manipulative. Maybe she put on her mask to show people what she wanted them to see, and to get her own way.

He'd had up-close-and-personal experience with the kind of woman who was shiny on the outside and all rotten core under the gloss. Annika had taught him a hard lesson. She'd shown him one side of her—exactly what he'd wanted to see—while her other, hidden side had almost killed him.

Logan shook his head, annoyed at himself. He walked along the airport corridor, and out the large glass windows, he saw the THS jet waiting on the tarmac.

It wasn't just Sydney Granger's tears that had gotten to him. It had been the way the woman had looked at his bare chest.

He'd seen heat and hunger. And that had made him feel something completely different.

He stopped near a door. "We'll wait here for Declan, Morgan, and Hale."

Sydney nodded. Her hair was still in its twist, but a few strands had escaped, falling around her face.

Shit. Now he was noticing her hair. Thankfully, at that moment, he saw Dec and the others coming toward them.

"Sydney, this is Morgan Kincaid." Logan pointed at the tall, deadly woman. Morgan was one of the best he'd worked with. She kept her dark hair short and had a scar down the side of her face she never talked about. The woman also had a big-time obsession with weapons. "This other guy is Hale Carter. Guys, Sydney Granger, our client."

Hale stepped forward with a smile. "A pleasure to meet you, ma'am."

As the man shook hands with Sydney, Logan rolled his eyes. Hale was a good-looking guy—dark skin, brown eyes, and a wide smile. He'd been a hell of a soldier, and now he was a hell of a security specialist. He was also a ladies' man.

"All right, let's get aboard," Dec said.

Logan stepped in front of Hale and pressed his fingers against Sydney's lower back. "This way."

Behind Sydney's back, Hale took a step back, holding his hands up in mock surrender. He grinned at Logan and winked.

They headed out onto the tarmac, and walked over to the sleek, black jet. Once inside, Logan directed Sydney to one of the plush leather seats. The jet wasn't outfitted for luxury; instead, it was lined with computer screens and compartments for storing their supplies.

Sydney settled into a seat, and Logan moved to talk with the others. But he felt her gaze on him the entire time. Once the pilot started the engines, Logan settled into the chair beside Sydney's. He wasn't sure why. He'd been telling himself he couldn't wait to get to the airport and hand her off to Declan.

Maybe he was just really keen to see a glimpse of that emotion again. To try and figure out the real Sydney Granger.

"What was your brother hoping to find in Peru?" Logan asked.

"He's obsessed with the Warriors of the Clouds. He said that only about five percent of their ruins have been uncovered in the cloud forests. He thinks there's much more to learn about them."

Morgan leaned forward from the seat behind. "What's so special about these Cloud Warriors?"

Sydney crossed her long legs. "Drew said that they were very advanced for the time."

"Oh?" Logan said. "Even though they didn't make metal?"

"The Inca were wary of them. Their warriors were famous in battle. Their shamans were feared. They mummified their dead and entombed them in fascinating sarcophagi that they lined up on rock ledges above canyons in the forests. Drew had been investigating evidence that they were advanced healers. He found evidence that they'd been performing bone surgery and successful amputations. He believed there was more about them that was still unexplored."

Logan grunted.

"Are you even interested in history?" Sydney asked, eyeing him.

"Sure." He enjoyed history, and it made him enjoy his job at THS even more. But he wasn't

24

dumb enough to fall for the old "lost city" and "lost treasure" fables. He'd been on too many expeditions that had come up empty-handed. He shrugged. "I like it. I like my work. The jobs are always different, and put my skills to good use."

"Holy cow," Morgan said. "Logan O'Connor likes something. Wow, hell must have frozen over."

Sydney turned and raised a brow.

Morgan laughed. "On every job, McGrumpypants is always bitching and moaning about something. Doesn't like the sand, doesn't like the jungle, doesn't like the mosquitoes."

"Ignore her," Logan growled. "I think she's taken too many hits to the head. I like my job, but Dec didn't hire me for my history knowledge."

Sydney's gaze ran down his body. "I guess not."

Logan ignored the faint hit of heat her gaze induced and shifted in his chair.

Morgan sat back and started watching a movie, and Sydney flicked through a magazine. Logan closed his eyes, figuring he'd catch some sleep.

"Why did you leave the SEALs?"

Sydney's quiet question made Logan tense.

"Sorry. Too personal?" she said.

He shrugged one shoulder. He glanced over and saw Morgan had her headphones on, and Hale and Dec were seated at a small table, playing cards.

"Dec had left—" and Logan had fallen for a pretty face and fucked up, big-time. He'd almost gotten his team killed. No way was he telling Sydney Granger that, though. "I guess I was ready for a change."

Sydney studied him for a long moment. She might be cool, but Sydney Granger wasn't dumb. She didn't push.

"You like being a CEO?" he asked.

Her face got a pinched look. "Jury is still out on that. My father died two months ago, and I'm still...finding my feet." She let out a sigh. "I'm not sure I'm cut out for this business thing."

"I guess it's a big change from going to Washington parties and hobnobbing." He hadn't meant it in a rude way, but he saw a flash of color on her cheeks.

"You don't know me, Logan." Then her face crumpled. "God, maybe if I hadn't been so busy with meetings and business dinners, Drew wouldn't be in this trouble."

This time, Logan didn't see a sheen of tears, or any flash of emotion on her face. But he felt it. Sydney Granger cared for her brother. "It's not your fault. Silk Road is to blame. We'll find him, Sydney."

She nodded.

Hell, Logan found himself wanting to pull her into his arms. To let her lean on him and for him to protect her.

Logan had never comforted anyone, in his entire life.

"Why don't you get some rest?" He stood, almost bumping his head on the low curve of the roof. "The seats recline."

He didn't look at her as he left to join the others.

Morgan had abandoned her movie and joined the

card game. She looked up and grinned. "Beauty and the Beast."

"The Ice Queen and the Huntsman," Hale murmured with a grin.

"Fuck you." Logan looked at Dec. "Any more info on why Silk Road has taken Drew Granger?"

Dec shook his head. "I asked Darcy to call Agent Burke. See if he has anything for us."

"Bet she'll love that." Special Agent Alastair Burke was head of the FBI's Art Crime Team. They were tasked with recovering stolen antiquities and artwork. Logan also knew the guy rubbed Darcy the wrong way.

"We've never heard of Silk Road taking hostages and demanding ransoms before," Dec added.

"They aren't short on money," Logan said.

"No. They aren't," Dec said, his brow creased.

So there was some other reason that Silk Road wanted Drew Granger. And why they wanted Sydney in Peru. Logan's gaze moved back to Sydney. Her eyes were closed and he let himself drink her all in.

He heard Morgan and Hale get up and head to the galley at the rear of the plane, arguing about what to eat.

Dec stepped up beside him. "You can't take your eyes off her, buddy."

"What?" Logan heard the horror dripping from his tone. "She's our client."

Dec crossed his arms and leaned back against the side of the plane. "Pretty easy on the eyes.

Those cool manners, pretty blue eyes, sexy long legs."

"You have a woman," Logan growled. When Dec just grinned at him, Logan suppressed the urge to hit something. "She's high society."

"Mm-hmm."

That small noise annoyed Logan to no end. "I hate when you make that sound, Ward. Look, you're in love, that's great. I like Layne, even if she has strange taste in men."

Dec slugged Logan in the shoulder, hard enough to hurt.

Logan narrowed his eyes and continued. "But don't go trying to pair me up with anybody. Especially with Sydney Granger."

"Mm-hmm."

Logan cursed. "I hate when you do that." He stomped back to his seat.

Chapter Three

It was still early in Denver, the day just beginning, and the air was crisp. Darcy Ward strode down the sidewalk, juggling her handbag, phone, and the latte she'd just bought from her favorite coffee shop. Their barista could work magic.

She took a sip and then huffed out a breath, watching the faint white puff of it in the air. Declan and the others would still be in the air but landing soon. She had to make this call...and it was late enough in D.C. now, so she was running out of excuses.

"Just get it over and done with, Darcy," she muttered to herself.

She lifted her phone and thumbed through her contacts. She found the one called *Agent Arrogant and Annoying* and hit the call button.

He answered after one ring. "Ms. Ward, this is unexpected."

That deep voice, that arrogant edge. Oh So Special Agent Alastair Burke did her head in.

"Agent Burke, I wish I could say it was a pleasure."

"But we'd both know you'd be lying. So why are you calling me?"

Darcy pulled a face, glad the sidewalk was empty. The man just couldn't be polite. She suspected he was a robot under his suits.

"I need some information—"

"You're asking me for a favor." His tone filled with amusement.

Ugh, if he was here, she'd throw her coffee at him. No, that would be a waste of good coffee. But she took a second to imagine him with coffee dripping off him. Tall, muscular body in one of his well-cut suits, brown hair, green eyes and the faint shadow of scruff on his cheeks giving him a dangerous edge. He'd tug his jacket off, displaying his shoulder holster and the wet shirt clinging to his well-defined muscles.

Darcy blinked, then went rigid. *Oh, no. No, no, no.* She wasn't going anywhere near that.

"It's about Silk Road," she said.

"What's happened?" Burke's voice sharpened and turned serious.

"We have a new client. Silk Road has abducted her brother down in South America and are demanding a ransom."

Burke muttered a curse. "Silk Road does not need ransom money."

She could hear his frown across the line. "That's what we thought, too. Have they ever done anything like this before?"

"No. This must be about something else. Usually something old, shiny, and priceless. Who's your client? What country did—"

"That's confidential." Darcy kept walking toward

the Treasure Hunter Security offices. She was smiling now. "Thank you for your help."

"You aren't going to tell me anything else, are you?"

"Nope," she said cheerfully.

"You still owe me." His voice deepened.

"I'll add it to Declan's tab." Her brother owed the agent several markers for past favors.

"No. I don't want a favor from your brother. I want it from you."

Darcy's steps faltered.

"You owe me, Darcy. And I will collect." The line went dead.

Darcy's smile disappeared. He was the FBI, so why did she feel like she'd just been threatened?

Damn the man. She'd changed her mind. If he was here, she *would* waste the coffee on him.

***

Sydney stirred, hearing the familiar low rumble that told her she was on a plane. Against her left side, she felt an intense warmth, and under her ear she heard a steady thump.

Opening her eyes, she looked up and realized she was leaning against a large, muscled man.

Logan.

She stayed there for a second, knowing she should pull away. But she didn't. He was asleep, and she let herself look at him. He looked no softer or tamer in sleep. She let her gaze drift across the powerful bridge of his nose, the rugged face, the stubble on his cheeks that made him look rough and tough.

His eyes opened—that brilliant antique gold—and for one humming moment, they stared at each other. Then they both pulled apart.

"Rise and shine." Declan appeared, holding two mugs of coffee. He handed them over. "Hope you slept well. We're just about to land."

Logan got up. Sydney clutched her coffee, and turned to look out the window. She saw the sprawl of the city below, and the strip of beach that separated it from the waters of the Pacific Ocean. She'd been to South America before, but never Peru.

The next few hours were a blur. They landed, then spent time clearing Immigration, waiting while the THS members' weapons and paperwork were checked over. Then she found herself being ushered into an SUV waiting for them outside the terminal.

From the driver's seat, Declan leaned back. "Darcy's booked us into rooms at your brother's hotel. Apparently, he paid for an entire month, and left some of his stuff there. We'll check in and then take a look at his room."

Wedged between Hale and Morgan in the backseat, Sydney just nodded.

It didn't take them long to get checked in. The Hotel San Antonio was in a lovely, white, colonial-style building. It was only two stories high, and each room had a small balcony with charming French doors.

Declan dropped her bag at her room before continuing down the hall. Sydney set her suitcase out of the way, and studied the lovely room, with its dark-wood floors, and the large bed covered by a crisp, white spread. Two couches and an armchair were arranged around an elegant wooden coffee table, and a narrow desk pressed against one wall. It wasn't long before there was a knock at her door. She opened it, and Declan, Logan, and the others piled into her room. Suddenly, the spacious room didn't feel so big anymore.

Declan sank into the armchair, Morgan took the couch, Hale leaned against a wall, and Logan prowled around like a predator. Declan leaned forward, hands resting between his knees. "I'm going to meet with the police. I want to see if there's any more information about the altercation that was reported. See if I can get a description of the people chasing him, exactly where they headed, and what happened." He spoke in a steady, confident tone.

Sydney could see he was easy with taking charge, and must have made a very good commander in the Navy.

"Morgan and Hale are going to go and check out the location of the chase and question any locals. Logan will take you to look at your brother's room and things." Declan's gray eyes were direct. "You know Drew better than any of us. You'll have the best chance of gleaning any information from his belongings."

Sydney nodded. She was quiet as she followed

Logan out into the hall. They took the stairs down to the lower floor. The hall was identical to the one above. Logan stopped in front of a door and pulled out a room key. "I'll check the room out first. You stay here." He reached under his shirt and pulled out a handgun. Sydney's eyes widened.

Logan slipped inside. Sydney shifted on her feet, waiting for him to come back. She didn't hear any noise, and the minutes seemed to stretch on, making her skin itch. Was he okay?

He was back a moment later, pushing the door open. Sydney moved inside.

The room was exactly the same as hers. The bed was neatly made and nothing looked out of place.

"There's plenty of his stuff still here," Logan said.

Sydney did a circle of the room, studying the empty surface of the desk, then the closet and the suitcase still stored inside. She fingered some of the shirts hanging in there. Drew favored polo shirts.

Pulling in a deep breath, she turned to Logan. "There's no laptop. He has one that he built himself. He never goes anywhere without it. He has a tablet, as well."

"There are some notebooks by the bed. Got some handwritten notes in them."

She saw where Logan gestured and spotted the plain black books. She flicked through them. They were filled with Drew's messy scrawl. On the chair beside the bed, she saw a discarded shirt. She lifted it up and smelled her brother's cologne. She closed her eyes.

"You really do care about him."

Logan's gruff words made her angry. "Of course I do. He's my brother. I may not shout all my feelings to the world, but I have them."

"So you lie. You show the world that bland, impassive face of yours, but inside you're thinking and feeling something else."

She released a sharp breath. "What I do and how I act is none of your damn business, O'Connor."

He shrugged a shoulder. "I just can't stand people who aren't what they appear to be. I can't seem to work you out."

He'd no doubt be shocked by what he didn't know about her background. She put on her frostiest voice. "You're not supposed to work me out, you're supposed to focus on finding my brother."

She turned around to do another lap of the room, looking for anything that she'd missed. She tried desperately to ignore Logan.

"Drew's clothes are here." She studied the contents of the closest again. "Based on the size of his suitcase, this is everything he brought with him." *God, Drew.* "He didn't have time or the opportunity to take any of it with him." What was Silk Road doing to him?

"Sit down." Logan's fingers curled around her arm, and he pushed her toward the armchair.

She bit her lip, trying not to cry. "You want emotion, here you go." She glared at him, feeling a lone tear track down her face. "Would you like a few sobs as well? Maybe some weeping?"

She heard Logan mutter. Then he knelt by her knees. "Don't you dare cry."

The words were harsh, but she heard the panic beneath them. A big, tough man like Logan intimidated by a woman's tears. It almost made her laugh. "You wanted to know if I felt anything—"

"No damn tears," he said again.

"God, you are so frustrating."

He touched her knee. "We'll find your brother, Syd."

"Don't call me Syd."

"I like it."

"You—"

Suddenly, the door burst open.

Sydney turned, saw bodies rushing in. Then bullets peppered the wall above them.

Logan yanked her off the chair and pulled her onto the floor. The air was crushed out of her lungs, and she couldn't have screamed if she'd wanted to. Logan's big body covered hers as more gunfire erupted around them.

***

Logan pressed down over Sydney. He lifted his head and saw shots thumping into the couch nearby.

Screw this. He reached down and pulled out his Desert Eagle pistol. He pressed his lips to Sydney's ear. "Stay down."

Logan sat up and fired back. But pinned down

like this, he couldn't get a decent shot at the intruders. They were hiding around the wall into the entry.

He got to his knees and then dived across the space toward the second couch. He heard more shots as he rolled and pressed himself flat to the ground.

He heard cursing, then footsteps. He rose up, firing.

The guy rushing at Logan dodged, his face covered by a black mask. A second man was following behind. He lunged and smashed into Logan. Together, they hit the coffee table with a loud *thud*. Logan wrestled the smaller man down and got on top of him. He slammed a hard punch into the man's face and the guy groaned. Another punch and the bastard fell back, out cold.

More gunshots. Logan's chest went tight. *Sydney*.

Logan fought the urge to stand up and rush in. He peered around the edge of the couch. Sydney was still behind the other couch, but a Silk Road thug was advancing on her, gun in hand.

Shit. But before Logan could move, Sydney reared up, a lamp clutched in her hands. She swung it hard and it slammed into the guy's head.

Hell, yeah. Then another guy rushed in from the front door and launched a hard kick into Logan's side.

Logan staggered and spun, and his gun flew out of his hand. *Hell*.

Anger flooded through his veins in a rush. He

grabbed his attacker, clenching his fists on the man's shirt. They spun, and then with a roar, Logan heaved the guy and tossed him toward the French doors.

Glass shattered. The Silk Road man screamed as he fell off the balcony. Logan was just sorry they weren't on the top floor.

He spun, and saw the other man grappling with Sydney. There was a trickle of blood down her cheek and her face was strained. The man was much larger than her.

Logan let out a growl and started in her direction.

Suddenly, Sydney dropped her weight back, and she and the thug stumbled forward. In a smooth, seamless move, she tugged the guy over her head. She dropped, and the guy crashed to the ground.

She leaped back onto her feet, and landed a sharp blow to the man's throat.

Logan let out a roar and charged. He grabbed the attacker and started pummeling him.

"Logan. Stop. *Logan*."

He kept up the hard punches, the rage inside him an animal thing.

"Logan." He felt a slim hand stroke his cheek.

He looked up at her.

"You need to calm down."

He worked his jaw, fighting down his battle haze. He dragged in a breath.

"You back?" she asked.

Chest heaving, he nodded. His gaze zeroed in on the nasty scratch on the side of her face. The smear of blood on her smooth skin was wrong. "He hit you."

"A slap. And you—" she cast a glance down at the groaning attacker "—pummeled him half to death. I'm okay, Logan."

"You sure?"

She nodded.

More in control of himself, Logan pushed to his feet, and his brain started processing what had happened. He pulled the zip ties he always carried out of his pocket and tied up their attackers. "Hell of a move with the lamp. And pulling him over your head. He must weigh twice as much as you."

"Guess I got lucky. Thanks to the adrenaline." She looked away and stepped back. "I'm glad I took those self-defense classes. They paid off."

She'd pulled herself together and now looked as cool as a glacier. She was also lying to him.

Memories of another woman—one who'd lied to him, duped him, and almost killed him and his SEAL team—roared to life in his head.

A bitter taste in his mouth, he advanced on Sydney and backed her up against the wall. Her back hit an abstract painting and it crashed to the floor. Her wide blue eyes stared up at him.

"Logan—"

He pinned her with his hands either side of her head. "Who the hell are you?"

"What do you mean?"

"Who. Are. You?"

The color had leached from her face. "Sydney Granger—"

"Stop lying." The words flew out of him like bullets.

"I'm really Sydney Granger, CEO of Granger Industries."

He thrust his face close to hers. "Enough. I saw you fight. All smooth and easy. No damn society clotheshorse moves like that."

"Self-defense—"

"Stop lying!" He couldn't stand to watch her lying to him. He saw her breath hitch. "Yeah, you should be afraid." He worked his jaw. "You're a foreign agent. Or you're undercover with Silk Road."

Her gaze snapped up. "What? No!"

"Who are you?"

She swallowed. "I am who I said I am, Logan. I can't discuss my...previous employment. It's classified."

He growled and yanked her away from the wall. Suddenly, her hands shot up, breaking his hold on her. She slammed an open palm into his nose. As pain exploded, he roared, and she tried to duck past him.

He grabbed her shirt and swung her. She flew sideways and hit the back of the couch. She kicked back with one leg, her boot hitting him low in the gut. He gritted his teeth and folded his body over hers, pinning her against the back of the couch.

She struggled against him, trying to get free, but he was too big and too strong.

Finally, she went still and heaved out a breath. "I was CIA."

Chapter Four

Sydney felt the anger pulsing off Logan's big body. "Can you get off me?"

"No." His lips brushed her ear. "You were sent to spy on us—"

"No, Logan. I don't work for the CIA anymore. I wasn't undercover and didn't often work internationally. I was under non-official cover. I planted surveillance devices on foreign businessmen and dignitaries suspected of criminal and terrorist activity. I was attending the right kind of parties and openings, and the Agency approached me several years ago. That's it."

"I had a pretty foreign agent sidle up to me once, all smiles and sexy innuendo. She said all the right things, swilled beer like a pro, played pool like a hustler, and sucked cock with abandon. I was an idiot and didn't see her lies until it was too late."

Oh, damn. Sydney squeezed her eyes closed. The hate and self-loathing in his voice scraped her raw. "I'm sorry. This was when you were a SEAL?"

She felt his chest heave against her. "Yeah. I was a sucker, but not again."

He pulled back and yanked her up. A second later, he tossed her over his broad shoulder.

"Logan!" She slapped her palms against his back.

He ignored her and carried her out of the room. He took the stairs two at a time, and stormed into his room. He dropped her into a chair.

Before she could do or say anything, he pulled some more zip ties from his pockets, and tied her hands to the arms of the chair.

"What?" She stared at her bound arms in disbelief.

"I have to deal with hotel security and the mess downstairs." His face had a hard edge. "Don't move."

He strode over to the phone and snatched it up. Soon he was talking in fairly good Spanish to what she guessed was hotel security. With his back turned, she tested the ties. They weren't budging. She sagged back in the chair. Damn, stubborn man.

It wasn't long before he set the phone down. He cast her one long look, then strode to his bag. Then he knelt beside her and opened a small first aid kit. He pulled out an antiseptic wipe and started dabbing at the cut on her cheek. She hissed out a breath, watching him steadily.

"It's not bad," he said, his voice like gravel. "Won't scar."

"I'm not really worried about that right now. Logan, I really was CIA and I really don't work for them now."

"Why'd you leave?"

She looked down at her bound wrists. "I left after my father died."

"You're still damn well lying to me."

She jerked her chin up. "You don't get to know every damn thing about my life. Now untie me."

He just stared at her.

"God damn you, Logan. My father died in a bomb blast at a hotel. The terrorist responsible…I was supposed to have planted a listening device in his room." The words felt ripped from her soul. "I hadn't found a way in…and my father died."

Logan stared for another second, then pulled out a large knife. Her pulse tripped, and then he very carefully cut her free.

She rubbed her wrists. Not looking at him.

"A terrorist killed your father, Sydney. Not you."

Oh, she knew that, logically. But sometimes, when feelings were involved, logic went out the window.

"Hey." He tipped her chin up. "It wasn't your fault."

Those simple words shouldn't have had such an effect on her. She stared at his shirt, and that's when she noticed that the side of his shirt was wet. His T-shirt was black, so she hadn't noticed before.

"Oh, my God, you're bleeding." She grabbed the hem and yanked it up. She gasped. "You've been shot!"

He shrugged. "Just a bit."

Panic skated through her. "You can't be a *bit* shot, Logan. I'm not a badass former Navy SEAL, but even I know this."

She tugged the shirt over his head and he grumbled as he let her. For a second, she was distracted by those muscles again. This close, she saw the scars marring his skin, including what looked like a previous bullet wound.

"It's not bad," he said.

He was right, it wasn't bad. The bullet had only grazed his side. She probed the wound gently. "Does it hurt?"

Golden eyes bored into hers. She suddenly realized how close they were standing to each other.

"No." He bit off a curse. "Don't look at me like that."

She felt the heat rising between them and swallowed. "Like what?"

"Like *that*." He grabbed her wrist and pulled her hand away from his chest. "I don't trust you."

Her heart skipped. Damn, that hurt more than it should.

But he lowered his head, their lips an inch apart, his face etched with struggle. Being so close to his big body made her feel so small.

The door slammed open. Declan strode into the room. "What the hell happened?"

Sydney and Logan sprang apart. As she smoothed her hair, she felt Declan's gaze on them. She knew what he saw—her disheveled state and Logan's shirtless chest.

"Silk Road paid us a visit," Logan said.

Declan swore. "You're both okay?"

"Logan fought them off. He got grazed by a bullet."

Logan looked at her. "Sydney held her own."

She looked up at him, surprised. She thought she heard the faintest of praise in his tone.

"That was when I discovered she hadn't told us the entire truth," he added gruffly.

Now, all she heard was acid. She turned to Logan. "I previously worked for the CIA. I didn't lie, it was *classified,* and no longer relevant."

Declan ran a hand through his hair. "Jesus. Okay."

Just then, Morgan and Hale arrived.

"All right," Declan said. "Let's all sit down."

"You running a strip show, O'Connor?" Morgan grinned at Logan. "If so, I'll make some popcorn."

Logan shot Morgan the finger and strode over to his bag. He grabbed some more things from the open first aid kit and started dabbing at his side. Once he was done, he slapped a bandage over the wound, and pulled on a clean shirt.

Sydney watched him, a part of her sorry to see him cover up. She let her gaze wander over his tattoos—that intriguing wolf, and those claw marks. When she turned her head, she spotted Morgan grinning at her.

Sydney sat on the end of the couch, moving her gaze to focus on something else. Like the beige wall.

"Darcy called. The FBI didn't have anything for us. I didn't find out much from the police report," Declan began. "I confirmed that the description of the man being pursued definitely matched your brother. One thing I did learn was that the group of men chasing Drew were all wearing black masks."

Sydney stiffened. "The men who attacked us were wearing black masks, too."

"Silk Road," Logan said darkly. "Drew's clothes and toiletries are still in his room. But Sydney says his tablet and computer are gone. And his room had definitely been searched."

Sydney looked up. "You didn't tell me that."

"It was a careful job. They wanted to make sure no one noticed."

Declan tapped his fingers on the arm of the chair. "Doesn't sound like he packed and left on his own."

Sydney's heart clenched.

"We found some notebooks." Logan pulled them out and dropped them on the coffee table.

Sydney leaned forward and opened the first one. "It looks like some of his notes and his research about the Warriors of the Clouds."

"Morgan, Hale, did you find anything?" Declan asked.

Morgan shook her head. "No one saw anything or they were too afraid to talk about it."

Sydney turned another page in the notebook. She stroked her finger over Drew's messy handwriting. No matter what kind of bribes their father had offered, Drew had never had neat writing. "He's got lots of notes and sketches in here." She studied some of the hand-drawn images. He'd always been a decent artist. He was just good at anything he tried. Her throat tightened. She couldn't lose her amazing, loving brother. She turned the page.

And froze.

"What is it?" Logan moved closer, sitting himself on the arm of the couch.

She realized that to most people, it would just look like more notes and doodles. But some of the sentences looked like gibberish. The letters were all mixed around and made up nonsense words.

"I think…" She looked up. "I think Drew may have left me a message. I need some paper and a pen."

A second later, Morgan dropped a hotel notepad and a pen in front of Sydney.

"When we were kids, we used to write each other messages in code. Drew invented it. I told you, he has a really high IQ. He loved puzzles and codes. This looks like one of those messages we used to write." She pointed to the section of gibberish.

She turned the blank notepad around and set to work trying to decode the message. It had been years since she'd done it, and she couldn't quite remember the process. She scratched out some words and tried again. That was better. She turned the page of Drew's notebook and spotted more mixed up letters. She started deciphering that.

She felt the others watching her and she kept going until she finally sat back, her heart pounding. She stared at the words she'd written.

Sis, bad guys after me. Want Cloud Warrior treasure. I've gone to Chachapoyas. Love you.

When had Drew written this?

"He's gone to the Cloud Warriors?" Logan frowned. "What does that mean, exactly?"

"Chachapoyas is also the largest town in the remote area where the Cloud Warriors lived. It's named after them."

"Damn." Logan's voice was a deep rumble.

She looked up. "What?"

She watched as he traded glances with Declan. It didn't take much to see that these two could communicate perfectly without any words. She'd never had a friend like that, and it was fascinating to watch.

"I think Silk Road attacked you because they want *you*," Logan said.

She frowned. "I don't follow. They demanded ransom—"

"They don't have your brother," Declan said.

She blinked. "But he's missing."

"Silk Road doesn't need money, Sydney. The ransom demand was just a way to lure you here." Logan pressed a hand to her shoulder. "I think your brother is onto some valuable discovery. One Silk Road wants. But I suspect he's given them the slip."

She sucked in a breath. "But what do I have to do with it?"

"Silk Road wanted you here so you could find Drew for them."

Sydney wrapped her arms around her middle. "We have to find him before they do. We have to go to Chachapoyas."

***

Logan bent and stepped out of the plane. He stopped at the top of the stairs and took a look around. Mountains, covered in fog, ringed the area. Chachapoyas Airport was small, with a single runway, and a simple white building serving as the terminal. The air here was cooler, but still pleasant. He slipped on his sunglasses against the bright sun.

Behind him, Sydney exited the plane. She was all put together, with a white shirt and fitted tan trousers. She looked like she'd stepped out of the pages of a damn fashion magazine. She certainly didn't look like a former CIA officer.

She slipped her own sunglasses on. "You're staring."

Ignoring her, he started down the steps. Near the terminal, two black SUVs waited. As always, Darcy was very efficient at organizing everything they needed.

Declan walked to the front SUV and opened the driver's side door. "We'll split up. Morgan, Hale, and I will take a look around the town, see if we can spot anything suspicious or any Silk Road members. Darcy managed to track down where your brother stayed when he was here. He rented a room at a small hotel in the town called Casa Andes. On the plane, I called the owner. He's happy for you guys to take a look at the room." Dec's face was serious. "Do you think your brother left you another message?"

"I hope so," Sydney answered.

"You and Logan go and meet this guy and take a

look. See what you can find." Dec cast a look at Logan. "Let's try not to smash or shoot up this hotel room this time."

"Wasn't me. It was Silk Road."

For an answer, Dec just slid inside his SUV.

Soon Logan was maneuvering his SUV through the light traffic of Chachapoyas. Sydney was looking out the window with interest. They passed the main square. It was lined with pretty white buildings with lots of arches, and topped with terracotta tiled roofs. A large, white church dominated the square.

"If circumstances were different, I'd really like it here," Sydney murmured. "I'd enjoy spending some time looking at all the ruins around the area."

Logan could think of better ways to spend his time off, but yeah, the town was pretty.

"I wouldn't think it was exciting enough for you. No high-society parties, and no secret CIA missions to pull off." He knew he was being a dick, but he couldn't help it. The fact she'd lied to him—even by omission—niggled.

She turned in her seat. "I get that you're still angry. But you need to drop it. My previous job wasn't relevant."

He grunted, and she turned away to look out the window again.

He pulled up near a three-story, cream-colored building accented with lots of dark wood. They got out of the car and walked toward the front door. The doors were also carved of dark wood, as were the window shutters lining all the windows.

They entered and from behind a desk, a cheery-looking local man bustled over.

"*Bienvenido!* Do you have a reservation?"

"I believe you spoke to my boss, Declan Ward. I'm Logan O'Connor, I'm with Treasure Hunter Security."

The man's smile widened. "Oh, yes. Your boss is a very nice man. He said that you wanted to see one of my rooms, just for a short while. Come, come." He waved his hands at them. "My name is Julio. I will show you."

He led them through another door, and it was then Logan realized that the building was a U-shape, with a central courtyard in the middle, covered in lush, green grass. Each floor was ringed by railings made of more dark wood.

Julio led them up some steps. He was eyeing both of them intently. "You are a lovely couple. You are sure you don't need my room for a night, maybe two?"

Sydney made a choked sound. "Oh, no. We are not a couple. No." She shook her head. "Absolutely not."

"I think he got the message," Logan grumbled.

Julio stopped outside one of the doors and pulled out a large ring of keys. "Really? Not a couple." He smiled at Sydney. "The big man watches you like you are his."

Logan's brows winged up. *What?*

But then, the man opened the door and waved them inside. "Take your time, take your time. I have lovely, clean rooms. If you change your mind and want to stay, I will give you a good deal." He headed back toward the stairs.

Logan turned his attention to the room. It was simple, nothing fancy. There were two beds with brightly colored covers—one double and one single. A dark wood desk with a spindly chair sat in one corner, and a solid-looking wardrobe was positioned against the back wall. As they looked around, Logan poked his head into the tiny bathroom.

Sydney checked the cupboard, the desk, and the bedside tables. She pulled open doors and drawers. Logan lifted the mattresses off the beds.

"There's nothing here," Sydney said bleakly.

"Look again. He must have left you something."

But a thorough search of the entire room and bathroom revealed nothing but a clean, sparse hotel room. She dropped down on the bed, her hands resting between her knees. "What do we do now? Do I need to search the entire Andes to find him?"

Logan heard the dejection in her tone. A part of him wanted to slide an arm around her, but he steeled himself against it. She may not have outright lied to him and the others, but she'd hidden a pretty important fact about herself. He wouldn't—couldn't—trust her.

"Your brother isn't a CIA agent too, is he?"

Sydney made an angry sound, and before Logan realized what she intended, she flew off the bed and slammed into him. Surprised, Logan fell, hitting the carpeted floor with Sydney on top of him.

He looked up and saw color flooding her face, anger in those pale blue eyes. Finally, the heat had burst through the ice. She trapped his arms against his body with her legs, her slim, but surprisingly strong, thighs clamping onto him.

"Listen to me, Wild Man. I may not have told you about my no-longer-relevant previous employment—"

"Feels relevant to me," he growled.

She jammed her knees into his side and he grunted.

Fuck. He was getting a hard on, and he was pretty sure that wasn't what she'd intended.

"I'm sorry you got duped and taken in. I'm sorry someone sent some redneck hottie that was right up your alley and you got fooled. Luckily for both of us, I am clearly not your type, and not what you want. You and I are chalk and cheese. I don't need some big, shaggy, bad-tempered alpha male in my face all the time. You got betrayed, Logan, time to get over it. If you were dumb enough to give away classified information to whoever was sharing your pillow, you need to learn from that mistake."

Logan gritted his teeth. "I never gave away classified information."

Sydney dragged in a breath. "Then why are you so twisted up about it, still?"

"Because I damn well gave her enough, and she made some educated guesses to fill in the gaps. My SEAL team was on a mission in North Africa and we were ambushed."

Sydney went still. "Logan—"

"No one died." God, he felt like the words were being torn out of him. He didn't even know why he was telling her this. "But a good man got a bullet in his spine, and he won't ever walk again. So I'm not going to just get over it."

"I'm sorry, Logan," she said quietly.

He so did not want to talk about this. When she shifted her body a little, she suddenly went still, her eyes widening. Yeah, she could hardly miss his hard cock jabbing her between her legs.

"Ah…" Heat was a pretty blush on her cheeks.

"You said you weren't what I want," he murmured. "You were wrong."

Her gaze met his. Her eyes were so wide, he could see the dark ring of blue around the paler color of her iris. At the side of her slim throat, he saw her pulse leaping.

Because he was an idiot, he bumped his hips up, grinding his cock against her. Her hands latched onto his shirt, twisting in the fabric.

"I can't damn well stop thinking about you," he growled. "I want to know what's lying under all that cool gloss of yours."

"This is a bad idea. You and I. No…just no."

"So why aren't you getting off me?"

She squeezed her eyes closed. "Dammit."

And in that one word, Logan heard what he needed. He reared up and slammed his mouth against hers. She moved her legs enough so he could free his arms. Her hands slid along his shoulders before moving to tangle in his hair. She kissed him back.

It wasn't slow or elegant. This kiss had an edge, the nip of teeth and the thrust of tongues. It was a battle, not a seduction.

Suddenly, she yanked her head back. She stumbled to her feet, pushing her tangled hair off her face.

"Sydney—"

"No. I don't want to talk about it right now. Later."

Logan dragged in a long breath, and jumped up. He tried to control the reaction of his raging body. "Syd."

"Let's just focus on finding my brother. That's what we're here to do." She turned away from Logan.

Job, lost brother. *Right.* "Your brother's smart, right? He's left a clue for you here. Somewhere."

"Maybe not at the hotel. Maybe somewhere else." She was frowning.

"Are there any other ways that he used to leave you messages? Like the codes you sent each other?"

Frustration etched her face. "The codes were the main way. And…"

When her voice just drifted off, Logan turned. "And what?"

"It's silly. He didn't do it often…it probably isn't anything."

"Try me."

"He used the mirror in my bathroom. He'd leave me little messages on it. He'd use soap and write a message and then clean it off enough that you wouldn't notice it. Then when the steam built up from the shower, the message appeared."

Logan strode to the bathroom. He flicked on the tap in the sink, running it on hot. He reached for the shower and did the same.

A moment later, steam started to fill the bathroom. Sydney stood beside him, her face tense, staring at the mirror.

Logan shoved his hands in his pockets. Hell, if a dedicated cleaner had been in here, they may have cleaned off whatever message Drew Granger might have left. Logan watched as the mirror began to fog up. They waited.

At first, he thought there was nothing there. Then he saw the letters appear like a ghostly message. It was a single word.

Kuelap.

Logan frowned. "What the hell is Kuelap?"

Beside him, Sydney beamed. "I remember it from Drew's notes. It's a Chachapoya site. It's not too far from the town, and a popular tourist destination."

"Okay, let me call Dec. We'll meet the others."

"Logan." She grabbed his arm and he felt her touch burn right through his shirt. "Thanks for not letting me give up."

He lifted his chin. "It's my job."

Her smile melted, and she nodded. "Let's go find the others and get to Kuelap."

Chapter Five

Sydney sat in the passenger seat of the SUV and tried not to fidget. But she was just so excited. They were getting closer to Drew, she could feel it. She pulled out Drew's notebooks and found the pages referencing the Cloud Warrior site of Kuelap.

Logan pulled the SUV to a stop near Chachapoyas' main square. A second later, the other SUV pulled up beside them. Logan and Declan lowered their windows.

"What did you find?" Declan asked.

Sydney leaned forward. "Drew left me another message. It was just one word—Kuelap."

"Which is?" Declan asked.

"The most famous of the Cloud Warrior ruins. It's about two hours' drive from here, and is perched on the summit of a hill. It's known as the Machu Picchu of north Peru. It's a fortress and walled city, the largest pre-Inca ruins in South America. It gets some tourists, but it's quite remote, so it isn't overrun like the more well-known Inca ruins in the south."

"All right," Declan said. "Looks like that's where we need to head next. You've got directions?"

"Yes."

"Any sign of Silk Road?" Logan asked.

"Nothing." Declan frowned. "I hate when there's nothing. Park your vehicle. We may as well just take one to see these ruins."

Sydney found herself pressed between Morgan and the window. Logan rode up front with Declan.

Sydney stared out the window as the town gave way to cleared patches of forest and small villages. In the distance she saw the mountains, covered in dense forest, and some with clouds hanging over them like a blanket. The very thing that had given the cloud forests their name.

She was cataloguing every little detail before she admitted to herself it was just a way to stop thinking about Logan. And that kiss. She looked forward, at the back of his head and broad shoulders. She was excruciatingly conscious of him.

That kiss. God, she should *not* be thinking about him. The man was too big, too annoying, too opinionated. She sighed. But a part of her was glad that he knew all about her, who she really was. She'd kept an important part of her life hidden from her friends, her father, even Drew. Most days she'd been okay with people thinking she was just a society woman who liked the arts and attending parties. But now, these people with her—honest, real, hard-working people who risked their lives to keep other people safe—knew who she was.

Logan knew.

Sydney tapped her fingers against her knee. She could understand why he'd been angry she hadn't told him about the CIA. That this foreign agent—

someone he'd cared about—had tricked him, used him. He must have hated that, and knowing a friend had been injured. A man like Logan wouldn't easily forgive himself for that.

It wasn't hard to picture the kind of woman who would appeal to Logan O'Connor. A woman with brash confidence, a body that never quit, and who was just a little wild.

Nothing like Sydney.

The others didn't notice she was quiet and lost in her thoughts. Their easy banter filled the vehicle. They acted like a big family—joking and teasing each other. Declan and Logan especially. The bond between them was clear to see.

It took them right on two hours to reach the base of the hill where the Kuelap ruins were located.

Declan got out of the car. "Looks like there's a kilometer-long walk up to the ruins." He was studying his tablet. "It says the path should be pretty easy going."

"You get signal up here?" Sydney asked.

Declan smiled. "I pay a small fortune for top-of-the-line satellite connections. Doesn't always work, but it's worth every penny."

Logan climbed out, looking at the few empty cars parked nearby. "Looks like they don't get too many tourists."

"Nothing like Machu Picchu, or Cuzco, or the Nazca Lines," Sydney said. "It's only been the last few years that the roads up into the north of the country have been improved, and more tourists have started venturing off the beaten track."

Sydney pulled on a light jacket. It was a little cooler up here, and she was grateful it wasn't winter. She could feel that the air was thinner and she needed to breathe deeper. The five of them headed off along the track leading up the hillside. The view in all directions was amazing—the deep green of the forests and mountains dipping down to the valleys below.

They walked up the track, moving into some trees. The walk was fairly easy, but she imagined if it rained, it wouldn't be much fun.

Sydney looked up as they cleared the trees, and the breath caught in her chest. "My God, it's amazing."

The top of the long, narrow plateau was ringed with a high stone wall. The walls had to be at least twenty meters tall, and to think it had been built by an ancient culture, hundreds of years ago. Seriously impressive.

Looking along the length of the wall, she saw a few places where the stones had tumbled down, but for the most part, she guessed sections of the wall looked as they had when the Warriors of the Clouds had lived here.

They kept walking, and ahead, she spotted an entrance through the stone walls. The narrow gap was only a few meters wide, flanked by the high walls. As she stepped through it, she felt like she was heading down a tiny alleyway.

Then she moved out into the citadel of Kuelap.

Wow. She'd always enjoyed history, and Drew's

ramblings on whatever latest culture he was researching, but this...she felt chills up her arms. Stepping into a place that practically echoed with the voices of the people who'd lived, loved, and fought here was amazing.

The remains of the ancient city spread out before them. There were lots of low stone walls, several in circles that outlined the bases of buildings. She saw lots of platforms and terraces at different heights to make use of the uneven land.

Drew's notes had mentioned that archeologists had found tombs and burials in parts of the site, filled with funerary bundles, ceramics, and the knotted strings known as quipus—used for recording information. And there was also an impressive drainage system.

"Split up and take a look around," Declan said.

Sydney nodded, and with Logan by her side, they headed in the opposite direction to Declan and the others. Ahead, she saw that one of the round buildings had been restored. The houses were circular stone walls topped by a cone-shaped thatch roof. She tried to picture all the buildings looking like this one. She imagined it would have looked reminiscent of a medieval village.

"My brother must have loved seeing this." Sydney carefully stepped over some tumbled rocks. "All this history that so few people see. When you think of Peru, you think of Machu Picchu and the Inca. The Warriors of the Clouds are forgotten."

Logan grunted, which she took for agreement.

They walked farther along the crumbling stone

walls. There were a few people dotted here and there. Sydney checked out everyone's faces, hoping to see the familiar blue eyes and smile of her brother.

But she didn't spot him. She reached a point at the outer defensive wall and stared down across the valley and to the mountains beyond. The view of the cloud forests, stretching out before her, took her breath away.

"Okay?"

She nodded at Logan. "I'm wondering what Drew stumbled onto that is so important that Silk Road would come after him." All she saw here were stone ruins. Amazing and of huge historical value, but nothing that she could think that Silk Road would want.

"Something valuable," Logan said.

She spun. "I've run my own searches. There is no mythical lost treasure of the Cloud Warriors. No stories of vast fortunes. No legends of cities of gold like in other parts of the continent. They didn't even make or use metal. Right here, at this very site, they've only found stone, ceramics, and fabric."

Logan stared at her. "And yet you said the Inca feared them. That they had the power to fight back against the greatest empire in the area."

Logan was right. The Cloud Warriors had something of value. And whatever it was had put Drew in danger.

Down in the ruins, she saw some local kids playing and laughing. They were dark-haired, and wearing brightly colored sweaters. As Sydney watched, she saw one girl staring in their direction. A second later, nimble as a gazelle, she ran toward them, leaping over the ruined stones.

As the girl reached them, she shot them a shy smile. Sydney blinked. The girl was maybe ten or eleven, and she had fair hair and freckles scattered across her nose.

Sydney went still. This girl was a descendent of the Chachapoyas.

"Señorita Granger?"

Sydney's back went stiff. "Yes. *Si*."

"*Para ti*." The girl pulled out a folded envelope and held it out. "He said you would be beautiful, tall, and have hair like mine," the girl said in Spanish.

As soon as Sydney took the envelope, the girl turned and went back to her friends. Sydney turned the envelope over. It was battered and covered in a smear of dirt.

"Sydney?"

She looked at Logan and held up the envelope. She tore it open, hope filling her. It was filled with papers.

She pulled the first one out and recognized the untidy handwriting. She shot Logan a blinding smile. "It's from Drew."

***

Logan sipped his beer. He sat beside Sydney and the team, huddled around a table in a restaurant in Chachapoyas. Dec had picked a table right at the back where they could keep an eye on anyone entering the restaurant.

So far, there had been no sign that Silk Road had followed them into the Andes.

But the back of Logan's neck was itching. They hadn't seen the last of the bastards.

Sydney's head was bent over the papers she had spread out on the table. He figured from the pinched look on her face, she wasn't finding what she wanted.

She sat back in her chair with a huff. "There's no message here." She shook her head, little tendrils of blonde hair curling around her face. "These are just articles on the Cloud Warriors that Drew must have printed out. He's made a few notations, but nothing that looks like a message."

"Tell us about the articles," Logan said.

Morgan rattled the ice in her glass. "Talking it out might help."

Sydney nodded and tapped one of the pages. "This article is about two silver cups dating from the Chachapoya era, and found at a Chachapoya site not far from here." She turned the page so they could all see the image. Two simple silver tumblers were engraved with images of people, and a geometric pattern.

Logan frowned. "I thought you said they had no metal."

"That's what the current belief is. Drew's made a special note of this discovery."

"Maybe they traded for these, or something," Hale suggested.

"The design is characteristic of the Cloud Warriors."

Dec set his beer bottle down on the wooden table. "So, let's recap. We have a mysterious, powerful people, who held out against the Inca, and who had no metal, while their neighbors were drowning in gold. And now these two cups have been found."

Logan lowered his beer and studied his friend. "You think they had metal."

Dec nodded. "Yeah. I think they did."

Sydney's eyes widened. "They were battling the Inca, but they knew the Inca had greater numbers. They must have known they were fighting a losing battle."

Morgan leaned forward. "And then the Spanish arrived, hungry for gold and treasure…"

"The Warriors of the Clouds hid their treasure," Logan stated.

"Oh, my God." Sydney gripped the edge of the table. "Drew put it together. And I bet he knows where this treasure is."

"And Silk Road wants it," Logan finished.

"What's the other article about?" Hale asked, from the other side of the table.

Sydney lifted the page. "It talks about the Cloud Warriors' unique burial practices. They created anthropomorphous sarcophagi out of clay for their dead. They were shaped like human bodies, with exaggerated jaws, painted white and decorated with other colors. The mummies were left inside and the most famous of these types of burials were lined up along a cliff face, facing out across the valley." She tapped her nail against a picture.

Logan studied it. The statue-like sarcophagi reminded him of small versions of the Moai statues of Easter Island.

"But another fascinating burial area of theirs was discovered south of here," Sydney continued. "Several mausoleums were found at a remote lake, high up on the cliffs. It's called Laguna de los Condores."

"Lake of the Condors," Logan said.

"It's also known as Laguna de las Momias."

Hale took a sip of his drink. "I don't speak Spanish, but even I can work that one out."

"There were about two hundred mummies entombed there. The six mausoleums, called chullpas, were built into caves on the cliff face above the lake. Unfortunately, looters attacked the site after its discovery, looking for treasure, and a lot of mummies were damaged."

"They find any treasure?" Logan asked.

She shook her head. "Archeologists removed the remaining undamaged mummies and artifacts. They're all located in a museum in the closest town. It appears the Cloud Warriors had advanced mummification techniques to preserve their dead from the humidity of the forest. And Drew's also noted that it appears mummification wasn't just reserved for the rich. Chachapoyans of all status were mummified."

Logan took another sip of beer. "You think this lake is where your brother headed next?"

Sydney frowned. "I'm not sure. Like I said, he didn't leave me a message. But it's all I've got."

Dec pulled his tablet out and set it on the table. He tapped the screen and a second later Darcy's face popped up, her headset settled over her dark hair.

Hale leaned into Declan's shoulder to look at Darcy. "Don't you have a life?"

Darcy pulled a face. "My life is keeping you guys out of trouble. What's happening?"

"Darcy, looks like we need to get to a place called Laguna de los Condores," Dec told her.

Darcy's brow creased and Logan heard her tapping on a keyboard. Then she groaned. "Well, you didn't pick the easiest location to get to."

"I know you like a challenge," Dec said dryly.

"It's just under a two-hour drive to the village of Leymebamba."

"Doesn't sound too bad," Logan said.

Darcy made a scoffing sound. "From there, it's a nine-to-ten-hour trek into the cloud forests. It looks like it's best to travel by horse."

Logan groaned. "I hate horses."

"You'll need decent gear for the trek," Darcy added. "And it looks like there is a local guide who takes the occasional tourist group up there. Let me get in touch with him." Darcy looked up. "And after this lake? Do you know where you'll head next?"

"No idea, Darce," Dec answered. "On this job, we're playing it by ear. It's likely we'll have to spend at least a few days in the forest."

Darcy nodded. "Leave it with me. I'll organize

gear for you to pick up there in Chachapoyas and then organize the guide and horses in Leymebamba. Give me at least an hour."

Logan shook his head. Only Darcy would only need an hour to find all the equipment they would need for a remote trek into the Andean cloud forests. But he knew she'd get it done. He'd seen her perform miracles.

"You're the best," Dec said.

Darcy winked. "Remember that when I ask you for a pay raise."

An hour and twenty minutes later, Logan was driving out of Chachapoyas, tailing Dec's SUV. Sydney sat quietly beside him, comfortable with the silence. He liked that she didn't feel the need to talk to fill the quiet. He hooked up his phone to the car and soon had some heavy rock pumping out of the speakers.

The road south wasn't particularly wide, but at least it wasn't dirt. If they met an oncoming bus or truck, it might be a tight squeeze. Looking ahead at the mountainous terrain, he figured there might be some scary drops off the side of the road in places.

"Your taste in music sucks," Sydney said.

He smiled. "Sorry, left my Mozart at home."

He saw her lips quirk. Then he noticed her hands were clenched in her lap. She was nervous about something.

He realized they hadn't had a moment alone since that wild kiss back at the hotel in Chachapoyas.

"Should we talk about the kiss?" she asked quietly.

Logan flexed his hands on the wheel. "I'm not much of a talker."

She looked at him with mock surprise. "No."

Smart ass. "Where have your polite society manners gone?"

Her face shut down. "I'm not some cold society snob, Logan." She crossed her arms and stared straight ahead out the windshield.

"I know," he said after a moment.

She turned to look at him.

"I worked it out sometime between discovering you're an ex-CIA officer, and seeing how much you care for your brother."

She swallowed. "I've lived my entire life with people only looking at the surface and making assumptions. Most people only see what they want to see."

And Logan had been guilty of that, too, when he'd first met her.

Because he wanted to, he reached out and touched her knee. "You're smart, Sydney. You have guts. And I've felt the heat you keep hidden." Hell, just the small taste he'd had of her was driving him crazy.

She stared at his hand resting on her knee. "You seem to ignite something in me, Logan." Her gaze met his. "Because I've never felt anything this hot before."

His fingers tightened on her knee. He didn't know what to say, but he knew what he wanted to do. But he figured pulling the car over, tearing her clothes off, and putting his hands and mouth all over her wasn't really an option at the moment.

"If we weren't in this car, on a mission to find your brother—" He let his words, and the promise in them, hang there.

She released a long breath. Then he noticed she was frowning, and looking out the window into her side mirror. Beneath his hand, her muscles tensed.

"Logan...there's a van speeding up behind us. It's coming in fast!"

Chapter Six

Sydney heard Logan's rough curse, his big hands clenching on the steering wheel. She watched as the white van got closer and closer. Maybe it was just some idiot driving too quickly on this narrow road?

They were slowly climbing up a hill. She glanced out at the steep drop next to them.

"Maybe they'll go past?" she said.

A second later, gunfire sprayed the back of their SUV. The back window shattered.

Sydney screamed.

"Down!" Logan roared and pushed her head down to her knees.

Sydney kept her cheek pressed to her legs and tried to calm her racing heart. She couldn't see what Logan was doing, but she felt the car wrench to the side. Then he accelerated and her seatbelt cut into her shoulder.

She lifted her head. There was more gunfire and more shattering glass.

"I said, stay down!"

She looked at him. "Give me a gun. I'll return fire."

"Stay. Down."

Annoyed, she reached over and delved into the waistband of his cargo pants. She felt the brush of warm skin and she heard him utter a curse. When her hand closed around the butt of his handgun, she pulled it out.

Sitting up, she turned inside her belt, aimed between the seats, and fired. The gun kicked back hard against her. She caught a brief glimpse of faces covered in black masks before the van behind them started to swerve.

She cursed. "You had to have a damn Desert Eagle." The gun was huge, and the recoil was a bitch.

She adjusted for the gun's kick and fired again. She was a bit rusty. She hadn't been to the range in a while.

Suddenly, the van's engine roared, and it shot forward, ramming into the back of their SUV. Sydney was jerked forward against her belt. She looked up and saw Declan's vehicle was executing a tight turn to head back in their direction.

"Hold on." Logan jerked on the handbrake, and suddenly the car was turning in a skid. Sydney's heart turned to a rock in her chest. The tires screeched, and she was excruciatingly aware that the road was narrow and the drop-off down the side of it was steep.

They came to an abrupt stop, rocking on their tires, facing the Silk Road van.

Logan punched the gas.

Sydney gripped the door. "What are you doing?"

"I'm going to distract them. Keep them focused

on us to let Dec do his thing."

The van was speeding up, too, coming straight at them. Her breath lodged in her throat. Logan jerked to the side, and they rode the very edge of the road. Their doors scraped against the other car. More bullets hit the side of their SUV, and Sydney returned fire.

They sped past each other, and Logan slammed on the brakes. He turned them again, in another sickening slide.

She saw the van slow and perform the same one-hundred-and-eighty-degree turn Logan had. It raced back toward them...apparently oblivious to Declan's SUV zooming up behind them.

Barely breathing, Sydney watched Declan's vehicle close in, and Hale and Morgan peppered the van with bullets.

The Silk Road van spun out of control.

Coming straight at Logan and Sydney.

She tensed. "Oh, God."

"Hold on." Logan tossed an arm across her chest.

The van smashed into them with a crash and a crunch of metal. Glass shattered. It felt like time moved in slow motion. Sydney felt the SUV slide closer to the drop-off into the valley. It was just feet away.

Then she felt the car roll.

They crashed onto the roof. Metal groaned. Then everything went still.

Sydney sat there, hanging in her belt, breathing hard. "Logan, next time I'm driving."

There was no response.

She turned her head and saw his body slumped, his eyes closed. There was no blood, but she saw a hard knot at his temple.

"Logan?" It was scary to see him so still and quiet. "Logan!"

Sydney reached down and undid her belt. She crashed down onto the crumpled roof of the car. Awkwardly, she managed to get her feet under her, and pushed herself out her broken side window.

Once out of the vehicle, she quickly circled around to Logan's side. Seeing how close they were to the edge of the cliff made bile rise in her throat.

She crouched. "Logan? Come on, Wild Man, we need to get out of here." She reached through the window and pushed his hair back from his face.

Then she heard a groan, and the crunch of a boot on broken glass. She frowned. Logan hadn't moved.

She spun. A Silk Road man stood above her, blood running down his face and soaking into his shirt. His black mask dangled around his neck. He had a gun aimed at her chest and blood smeared on his teeth. "You're coming with me."

Sydney looked back and saw Dec's vehicle wheeling around, coming back toward them. "There's nowhere to go. You should run before they get here."

"I'm more afraid of my employer than them."

He reached down, grabbed her arm, and yanked her to her feet. Sydney tried to stay calm. Then the man swiveled, raising his gun to her right.

Right at the still-unconscious Logan.

Her gut hardened and she gathered herself. *No*

way. She turned and rammed her shoulder into the man's gut.

He stumbled back with a cry.

And the gun went off.

***

The gunshot echoed in Logan's ears. He felt the crunch of glass under his hands, and the hard press of a seatbelt across his chest.

For a second, he was back with his SEAL team, after they'd been ambushed. He was trapped in the Humvee, his injured friends' screams and gunfire echoing around them. Along with the sickening realization that they'd been ambushed—and Logan had instantly known the source of the leak. Fucking Annika had screwed him over in more ways than one.

But as he opened his eyes, the past faded. He realized in an instant where he was.

He turned his head and saw Sydney struggling with a man.

Logan wrestled the seatbelt off, and, grunting, he moved to get out of the crumpled vehicle. He felt glass scratch down his arm but he ignored it. He shoved at the door, but it was so bent out of shape that it wouldn't budge.

He shoved again, and, with a roar, he gripped the frame and started to strain against the metal. He kept pushing, using all his strength, and he felt the metal bend. A second later, he gave the door another hard shove and it opened. He rolled out of the car.

Logan jumped to his feet, ready to help Sydney.

He came to a stop.

She already had the guy down. He was groaning, holding his bloody face, and writhing on the road.

Sydney stood there, cool and calm. The air sawed in and out of Logan's lungs as he tried to calm himself.

"Hey, it's okay." She moved up close to him, studying his face intently. "You're all right?"

He managed a nod.

She reached up and tentatively touched his chest, stroking.

"You're not hurt," he managed to get out.

"No. I'm fine."

Because he needed it, Logan yanked her to his chest. She went still for a second, then softened against him, her arms creeping around his waist.

There was a squeal of tires, and the other SUV skidded to a stop next to them.

Dec, Morgan, and Hale rushed out of the vehicle. Dec eyed the crashed SUV, then the wreck of the Silk Road van, and the unmoving bodies of the other Silk Road members inside. Finally, his gaze rested on the thug writhing on the ground.

Dec rubbed his chin. "Hale and Morgan, check the men in the van. Tie them up if they're still alive." Dec looked at Logan. "You guys are okay?"

"Yeah." Logan eyed the man. "Maybe he's not feeling so good, though."

A faint smile crossed Dec's face. "We'll push the

wrecks off the road and then I'll get Darcy to call the authorities. You two get in the vehicle."

"We don't need to stay?" Sydney asked.

"No. If we get tied up with the authorities, we'll be here for days. Darcy will sort things out with them." He pulled out some black zip ties. "We'll leave these guys secured and let the police deal with them." He frowned at Logan. "Logan, you're bleeding."

Logan heard Sydney gasp and pull away from him. He shrugged. "It's just a scratch."

She studied the nasty cut on his arm from the glass. "You call that a scratch?"

He smiled crookedly. "Sure. You wouldn't?"

"How's that knot on your head?"

"Fine. I've had worse."

"And you have a hard head."

Dec and the others made short work of shoving the wreckages to the side of the road, and grabbing the gear from Logan's vehicle. As they climbed back into Dec's SUV, Logan made sure that Sydney was sitting beside him in the back. He let her fuss over him, pulling things out of the first aid kit, and swiping the blood off his arms.

"You look like you crawled over glass," she muttered.

"I was trying to get to you."

Her hand stilled for a moment, then she kept wiping. "Despite what most people think, I can take care of myself."

"Never thought you couldn't."

"This one's deep here. It could do with a bandage."

"Here you go." Declan passed something back from the front seat.

Logan saw Sydney take the small Band-Aid and then her mouth moved into a smile.

"This is pink. With princesses on it."

Logan made a grumbling sound and crossed his arms over his chest. "Declan thinks he's a comedian sometimes."

She held the small strip up, eyeing Logan's arm.

"Don't even think about it."

The car erupted with laughter, easing the tension.

The rest of the drive to Leymebamba was uneventful. The only vehicles they passed on the road were local vehicles, and a pair of tourists riding motorbikes.

They pulled into the quiet town of Leymebamba. It was nestled in a valley, the mountains rising up around it. The narrow streets were lined by simple buildings with tiled roofs.

Dec pulled the vehicle to a stop and turned back to look at them. "Darcy's got us rooms at a local hotel. There's not much to choose from here, so the rooms are basic, but they'll do. I need to go meet with a local guide. He's organizing the horses we'll use for the trip to the lake. We'll leave first thing in the morning."

"I hate horses." Logan spotted Morgan rolling her eyes and scowled at her. "So will we meet up for dinner?"

Dec nodded. "Take the chance to have a long shower, soak in the tub. We won't be getting much of that once we head into the forest. We all need a good night's sleep. Tomorrow is going to be hard going."

Soon, Logan found himself carrying his duffel bag into his hotel room. Basic was being generous. The walls were bare and white, and a single bed occupied the space. He snorted. He was sure his feet would hang over the edge. He looked out the window and saw a central courtyard filled with a variety of lush plants. A bird feeder hung from the roof and a hummingbird flitted around it.

He dumped the bag and stripped off his clothes on the way to the tiny bathroom. There was a tub. Although he'd never admit it to Declan, Logan liked soaking in the tub. He turned the water to run as hot as he could get it and then sank into the water.

He let his head drop back, resting against the plain white tiles. With his eyelids closed, he kept seeing that van ramming them from behind, hearing the bullets hitting the car, and then the sickening lurch of the crash.

Dammit. Sydney could've been killed. *Fucking Silk Road.* Logan focused on the anger. It was a far more familiar and easier emotion to deal with than the other, confusing emotions that he had in him for Sydney Granger.

He thought of Annika again. She'd burned hot and bright. She'd had a dirty mouth, was aggressive in bed, and he'd believed she was his dream woman... Or so he'd thought.

None of it had been real. And yet, with Annika, he'd never felt a fraction of the desire he felt for Sydney. Hell, since he'd met her, he'd been walking around half hard. Sydney was a cool, crisp breeze, one that hid a healthy, sexy and very real fire beneath.

His bathroom door slammed open.

"Logan!"

Sydney came to a halt in the doorway, staring at him.

She pressed her hands together. "I knocked on the main door. When you didn't answer, I got worried. I thought you'd passed out or something."

Logan just stared at her. She'd been worried about him? He tried to remember the last time anybody, especially a woman, had worried about him. Most people expected him to worry about them. Hell, it was his job to protect others.

He took her all in, noting the pink in her cheeks and her fresh clothes. He saw that her gaze was nowhere near his face. The water of his bath didn't hide anything.

She cleared her throat. "How's your head?"

He snorted. "Which one?" She could hardly miss his raging hard on.

She lifted her chin. "Sounds like you're fine." She took a step backward.

"Don't." His voice echoed off the tiles.

She stopped. "This is a bad idea."

Probably. "Come here, Sydney."

She shook her head. "We're here to find my

brother. Silk Road is after us—"

"Seems to me that you've been doing everything for everyone else for a really long time. When do you get to do what you want?"

She fell silent.

"You've helped your country, which meant hiding who you really are from your family and friends. It's tough when you have to keep that part of yourself separate. You're learning to run your company for your dad. And you're down here in South America, in the middle of nowhere in the mountains, for your brother. What about you, Sydney? What do you want?"

She stood there, her slim body vibrating. "Sometimes we don't get what we want."

"And sometimes you've just got to reach out and take it."

She took a single step and stopped.

"What do you want, Sydney?"

She shivered. "You."

"I'm all yours."

She closed the distance to the tub, dropping down on her knees. "I want…I want to touch you. I thought that Silk Road guy was going to kill you today on that roadside."

Logan wanted to lunge up and grab her, but he forced himself to stay still. He'd meant it. He wanted Sydney to finally take something for herself, not be always giving and subduing her own needs in the process. He forced himself to stay still, his hands curling under the water.

She reached out, her slender fingers brushing

against his chest. She let them drift over his shoulder, skirting the small cut marks. She reached his tattoos at the back of his biceps and stroked each one with a focused attention that made more blood race to his cock. Then her hand drifted down again over his chest, lower, running over each ridge of his abdomen.

Now Logan was breathing hard.

"You're magnificent," she said quietly.

He knew that in his entire thirty-five years of living, no one had ever called him magnificent. And no one had ever said it and believed it like Sydney.

He lunged up and grabbed her. She gasped. Naked and wet, he carried her through into the bedroom. He tossed her on the bed, towering above her.

She stared up at him and he saw her chest rising and falling rapidly. Desire flared in her eyes—bright and hot. Her gaze drifted down and locked on his very engorged cock.

Logan lowered himself on top of her. He pressed his lips to hers, driving his tongue inside her mouth. He needed the taste of her. He needed the feel of her. She kissed him back eagerly.

As he devoured her, her hands slid down his sides, and a second later, he felt her slim fingers close around his cock.

He groaned and thrust himself into her hands. "You want me inside you?"

"Yes," she panted. She stroked him again with firm, hard pumps. "You're a very generous handful, Logan. I can't wait for you to be inside me. To watch you lose control."

He groaned again. Then he heard a knocking sound.

It took him a second to realize that someone was knocking on the door.

"Ready for dinner, O'Connor?" Declan called out.

Hell. Logan felt his entire body trembling and he fought for some control. But Sydney didn't stop her caresses. She sped up her strokes and he felt the start of his orgasm coiling at the base of his spine.

He'd never had sex like this. Him naked, a woman clothed and giving him pleasure.

"Give me a minute." He wasn't sure if Dec would be fooled. Logan lowered his voice "Syd—" His words ended on a tortured growl.

"So big, so hard." She kept working him. "I want you to come for me, Logan. Right here, right now."

He groaned, trying to keep it quiet, since he knew Dec was only feet away and separated by thin wood. Logan was usually loud during sex. He'd never been forced to keep his control like this, to contain his response. For him, sex was always fast and a little wild. This was different, and agonizingly amazing.

She stroked faster, and he kept pumping his hips into her hand. She reached down and cupped his balls.

Logan stiffened and came with the force of a freight train. She pulled the sheet up to cover the head of his cock, and instead of roaring out his release, he buried his face in her throat, his lips pressed against her skin. He opened his mouth and gently bit her, catching that sensitive tendon between her neck and shoulder. She arched under him with a fierce, quiet moan.

"Don't have all day, O'Connor," Dec called again.

Chest heaving, Logan tried to get his brain firing. His body was still humming with pleasure and his legs felt numb.

"Go," Sydney whispered.

He pulled back to look down at her. Flushed cheeks, swollen lips, and a very satisfied look in her eyes. Damn, he wanted her. He didn't care about dinner or his best friend. He wanted to lodge himself inside her and take all night to explore every luscious inch of her. Find out what she liked, what made her cry out, what made her blush, and what made her come.

"I'll see you at dinner, after I clean up," she said.

Dec pounded on the door again. "We have details to sort out for tomorrow. Quit snoozing, Logan."

Logan closed his eyes for a second and raised his voice. "I just finished washing up. Give me a chance to get dressed."

He gave Sydney one last and frustratingly short kiss, before he stood. "Later."

She smiled. "Count on it."

Chapter Seven

Early the next morning, Sydney found herself seated on a horse, riding up the mountainside above Leymebamba. The sun was shining, and the air was crisp and fresh. The view back down to the village in the valley was gorgeous.

The others were riding ahead of her. She stared at Logan's back. He'd grumbled about getting on the horses that the local guide had brought them, but of course he rode with an easy rhythm.

The local guide, Piero, was chattering away in Spanish to Declan.

"I take tours to the lake, but very few come." He had a friendly face and dark hair. "The mummies are now all in the museum in the village. But the lake is very beautiful. I wish more people wanted to visit it."

Sydney smiled to herself. She couldn't imagine too many tourists wanted to do the strenuous ten-hour trek to Laguna de los Condores. Her gaze drifted back to Logan.

Instantly, she thought about what they'd done in his room. She bit her lip, a shot of heat arrowing between her legs. Man, it was so easy to imagine his hands on her skin, his very mobile mouth moving over hers, and that very large cock in her hands. She huffed out a breath, squirming in the saddle. Now was not the time to be thinking about this.

She'd come here for Drew...not to become a little obsessed with a big, sexy man.

After their sexy little moment, he'd headed off with Declan while she'd cleaned up. She'd met them all at the tiny restaurant and they'd shared dinner. They'd spent the entire time planning today's trip and eating the simple but delicious food. Logan had kept sending her heated, intense looks from under hooded eyes, and she'd had to use every ounce of her skill at keeping her face impassive.

Sydney had wanted nothing more than to drag him back to her room and strip him naked. But after dinner, Declan had wanted Logan to spar with him. Then he'd looked Sydney straight in the eye and told her to get a good night's sleep in advance of today's trek. She suspected Declan had known exactly what was going on in Logan's room earlier.

She wanted Logan. She gripped the reins harder. She'd never felt this kind of out-of-control desire, or this kind of connection with a man before.

How could someone who seemed so wrong feel so right?

At that moment, he looked back over his shoulder. His intense gaze was like a physical thing. Despite the cool air, heat prickled over her skin. It was like he looked right inside her. No walls, no pretense, no polite society manners. Just raw, primitive want.

But as they continued into the cloud forests, the journey got more challenging. She had to focus on maneuvering her horse along the narrow dirt track. The trees of the cloud forest weren't massively tall, and they had gnarled trunks and branches. She knew the higher altitude of the cloud forests changed the characteristics of the trees. Lots of lichen, moss and ferns grew as well. At times, the dirt path was very narrow, the drop-off down the hillside breathtaking. A few times, they had to climb off the horses and lead them through rougher patches of the track.

After a couple of hours, they stopped for a rest.

Logan appeared by Sydney's side. "Okay?"

"My behind is not happy," she said.

Something flared in his eyes and he leaned down, his lips brushing her ear. "I'll be happy to rub it for you later."

She swallowed. This man was dangerous. A wild, stalking predator who'd devour her whole if she wasn't careful.

"Logan—"

He reached out and fiddled with her hair. "Every time I look at you...I want you even more."

She released a breath. It was strange to hear the sweet words uttered in that gruff, deep voice. So at odds with the wild desire she saw boiling in his gold-brown eyes.

"Chalk and cheese," she muttered.

He grinned at her. "I like cheese."

She snorted. "The sort that squirts out of a can, right? Onto your nachos?" She shook her head. "I like fine wine and Camembert."

His smile widened. "There's no fancy French wine and cheese out here, Princess. Just you and me. Besides, don't knock my cheese until you try it."

A reluctant laugh broke out of her.

Declan called out. "Everyone, Piero says we need to keep moving. We want to reach the lake before dark."

They kept moving through the forest. At the next break, Logan and Declan were huddled over a map. Sydney stared up at the overgrown trees and the vines hanging off them. She tried to imagine Drew making this trip. Maybe he'd sat right here to rest. *Please be okay, baby brother.*

Piero wandered over to check her horse. "Piero, have you seen an American man in your village lately? Over the last few days?" She was a little out of practice with her Spanish, but it was passable.

The man frowned, his dark brows drawing together. "Mr. Declan asked me already. There have been a few tourists." He lifted one shoulder.

"You haven't guided a man to the lake recently? He's about six feet tall, slender, blond hair like mine—?"

Piero's frown deepened and he shook his head. "No. Sorry, *señorita.*"

Sydney's shoulders sagged. She knew it had been a long shot.

Piero stroked his chin. "Maybe I saw a man like you have described in the museum. There was a tourist with blond hair."

Her pulse leaped. "But he didn't ask you to take him to Laguna de los Condores?"

"No."

"*Gracias*," she replied.

Piero eyed her for a second, then flashed her a smile, and patted her horse. He took a moment to fiddle with the saddle and then moved back to his own animal.

As they continued on, the journey lost some of the shine and excitement. Monotony set in and her muscles started to ache. The beauty of the forest and the mountains, and the occasional layers of cloud she saw lying over it, had worn off.

Sydney's horse started playing up—fidgeting, disobeying her commands. He started lagging behind the others.

She noticed Logan look back at her again.

"I think my horse is unhappy." She couldn't blame the poor thing.

Piero dropped his horse back. "I will check it." He waved to the others. "Go on. We will meet you at the rope bridge that is just ahead. I must cross it first."

Sydney climbed off her horse, massaging her thighs. She was going to be sore tomorrow. She watched Piero as he stroked her horse, clucking to it softly.

She turned and stretched. She was definitely going to be happy to see the end of this journey.

And she'd be even happier if it ended with her brother safely back with her.

Suddenly, a hand slammed over her mouth. She felt the prick of something sharp at her side, digging through her clothes. She looked down and saw a large hunting knife. Her heart knocked hard against her ribs.

"You will listen to me." Piero's easygoing tone had vanished. He was speaking in perfect English with the faintest touch of an accent that wasn't South American. "You do as I say, and the others in your group won't get killed."

***

On her horse, Sydney approached Logan and the others.

She schooled her features to blandness, like she had thousands of times before at Washington parties, or when she'd been sneaking surveillance devices into offices or hotel rooms, or lately, when she faced the board.

But something that had been so familiar to her now felt so wrong.

Funny. Over the last few days, around the Treasure Hunter Security team, around Logan, she'd gotten used to laughing, trading barbs with Logan, and showing her emotions. She'd felt like herself.

No. She stiffened her spine. She couldn't afford to let her emotions leak through. She had to put on that mask and lie to protect the people around her.

She sensed Piero, or whatever the hell his name truly was, move his animal up directly behind hers.

Against her chest, she felt the small device he'd shoved inside her shirt. The tiny thing felt like it weighed a ton. He'd said that it was a high-powered explosive, and if she didn't follow his orders exactly, or she tried to warn the others, he'd kill her.

And he'd smiled as he'd promised that the blast would injure whoever was standing close to her.

Sydney ran her gaze over Logan's strong form, drinking him in one last time. As it always did, desire rose, but she stamped down on it.

When Logan turned her way, she shifted her gaze and slid off her horse. She was sure he'd read her like an open book if he got a good look at her face.

"How's the horse?" he asked.

"Fine now," Piero answered. "There is the bridge."

Sydney's stomach clenched. The bridge hardly looked sturdy enough for a child to cross, let alone a full-grown adult and a horse.

The rope bridge was suspended across a long chasm between two mountains. It wasn't a super long drop to the river below, but long enough. The sides of the drop were steep and rocky.

"The Inca were well known for their rope bridges," Morgan said.

Piero nodded. "There are many rope bridges in the remote hills. We replace them when they start to wear. Luckily, we can use modern rope now." He smiled. "Much sturdier."

His "easygoing guide" persona was back in place. Sydney tried not to glare at him.

Sydney looked at the bridge again. The base of it was reinforced with wooden planks, but she could see small gaps between them. Her stomach did a sickening turn. She wasn't afraid of heights...usually.

"I'll go first to test it," Piero said. "We will have to go one at a time with our horses. But don't worry, my friends, the bridge is very strong."

He'd ordered Sydney to stay close and to ensure she was the first person across after him. She moved closer to the edge, pulling her horse behind her.

Logan's shoulder brushed against hers. "I'll go next," he said.

She shot him a bright smile. "I want to let my inner adventurer loose, Logan. I'm going next."

He didn't smile as his gaze traced over her face. She turned away, and saw Piero and his animal step off the other side of the bridge. Sydney pushed forward, stepping onto the swaying bridge, leading her horse out behind her.

Sydney gripped the rope on one side and simply focused on putting one foot in front of the other. She didn't look down, she didn't look back. She stared ahead and saw Piero's dark eyes on her. Once she neared him, she saw him pull out his knife and start sawing through the rope tying the bridge to the rocks on the other side.

She slowed, panic filling her. She wracked her

brain for a way out of this. Then she saw Piero pat his chest—right over the same spot where he'd put the small explosive on her. The device felt like it was burning through her skin, even though it was cool to touch.

She stepped off the wobbly bridge onto the ground. Piero nodded, and Sydney pulled in a breath and turned.

She raised her voice. "I'm afraid this is where we part ways."

On the other side of the gorge, the THS team froze.

"What?" Logan demanded. His gaze zeroed in on Piero who was busy cutting more ropes. "What the hell is he doing?"

"I should never have contracted your services." Sydney struggled to find her best CEO voice. "I need to find Drew on my own. Thank you for bringing me this far."

Logan stepped out onto the bridge. "Syd, what the fuck is going on?"

She tried for a bright smile. "I'll pay the agreed amount." She forced herself to look at Logan.

"Make it convincing," Piero murmured.

She swallowed. "I no longer need your services."

She could hear Declan and the others whispering. Inside, she felt like she was being sliced to pieces. Piero cut through one side of the bridge and the entire thing lurched to the side. Logan reached out and grabbed onto the ropes, holding himself upright.

Oh, God. If he fell... She willed him to move off

it, but he didn't. Stubborn alpha male.

"Sydney, talk to me—"

His tough, gravelly voice scraped over her. "There's nothing to talk about."

The stubborn man took another step forward. Her heart leaped into her throat. "No! Don't come any closer."

With grim determination etched on his rugged face, Logan took another step toward her.

Her heart was thundering now. She knew he wouldn't give up, knew he'd keep coming for her. Unless she made him stop.

"I don't need you anymore." She put on her haughtiest face.

He went still.

God, she was being torn in two. "You got me this far. I can take it from here." She forced out a light laugh. "You didn't really think I could want a man like you, did you?"

His gaze was boring into her.

She could guess what he was thinking and feeling.

She was just another liar like Annika.

Hell, maybe she wasn't that different. He'd confided his worst moment to her, and now she was turning it back on him. "You've served your purpose, Logan. Go home. I don't want or need you."

Piero cut the last rope.

The bridge fell, and Logan with it.

Sydney slammed her fist against her mouth to stifle her scream. Logan grabbed on with both hands. As the bridge slapped against the other side, hanging vertically, Logan also clung there, hanging above the drop.

Fear was jagged claws in Sydney's belly. He was okay. He was holding on and climbing up the ropes. She saw Declan and Hale reaching down to pull him up.

"Come." Piero grabbed her arm, his fingers digging into her skin. He yanked her away.

Sydney looked as long as she could, wanting to make sure Logan was safe. As soon as she saw the others pull him over the edge, her tight chest eased.

And then Piero tugged her into the trees, cutting off her view of her friends.

Chapter Eight

What. The. Fuck.

Logan paced back and forth, his boots kicking in the dirt. As he prowled, he stared across the gorge at the wall of trees where Sydney had disappeared.

Not far away, Morgan was studying their map.

"Logan."

Dec's calm voice was like sandpaper on Logan's nerves. "What?"

"Are you okay?"

"No." At first, he'd been confused. Then, as Sydney's words had hit him like a rain of automatic gunfire—well-aimed fire—he hadn't known what to think.

For a second, it had felt like Annika all over again.

Until he'd really looked at Sydney.

Hell, he'd been watching her nonstop for days, ever since she'd stepped into the Treasure Hunter Security warehouse. He'd gotten pretty good at reading her face. As she'd stared across that bridge, her face had been blank, composed, a mask. Her tone had been cool as icy rain. And she'd refused to meet his gaze for more than a few seconds.

From the moment he'd met her, Sydney Granger

had never been afraid to look him in the eye. But that entire time she'd given them her little speech, she'd avoided eye contact.

With a frustrated roar, Logan ripped at some vines dangling from the nearby trees. He tore the plants into tiny pieces. It wasn't enough. He slammed his fist into the trunk of the tree, again and again, until his knuckles were bloody.

Dec crossed his arms over his chest. "Feel better?"

His best friend had seen him lose it too many times to be alarmed. "No. Something's wrong. Silk Road got to her."

Fear was ice in his veins, and it made him angry. Silk Road had Sydney. She was in danger. Logan stared across the chasm. "We have to get to her, Dec."

Dec released a breath. "Good. I'm thinking the same. I wasn't sure you'd…"

When his best friend broke off, Logan raised a brow. "You walking on eggshells around me now, Ward?"

"What happened with Annika fucked you up. You've never trusted a woman since. Or yourself with one."

Logan was starting to feel the sting of his torn knuckles. "Sydney would not have left like this. She wouldn't have said those things."

"You sure? She's a millionaire heiress, a CEO, and a society girl. She doesn't really move in your circles, Logan. Not to mention her past with the Agency. She could be fooling all of us."

"She's not!" Logan's shout echoed around them.

Dec smiled and nodded. "That's what I think, too. I just wanted to make sure your head was screwed on right."

"Bastard," Logan said, but there was no fire in the word.

Together they turned to Hale and Morgan. "How are we going to get across?" Dec asked.

Morgan tapped the map. "There's a spot where we can cross downstream, but it's a long way out of our way, plus there's no track. We'd have to hack through the trees. It'll put us far behind them."

Hell. Logan didn't want Sydney being in the hands of Silk Road any longer than she had to be. If he hurt her, Logan would make him pay. "Too long."

Hale pulled his backpack off the back of his horse. "I have an idea."

Logan watched as Hale pulled something from the bag. It looked like a gun, but as Hale extended it out and pressed a button on the side, Logan saw a sturdy grappling hook slide out of the end.

"I've been wanting to test this little baby out," Hale said.

It was a grappling gun, but the most compact one Logan had seen. He'd used other ones on SEAL missions, but they were big, heavy, and not portable like this one. Hale lifted it and aimed across the chasm. He pulled the trigger.

It wasn't very quiet, making a loud whistling sound as the hook and line whizzed through the air.

It flew across the gorge and slammed into the rocks on the other side.

Hale pulled back on the line, testing it. "Ladies and gentlemen, we have a sturdy, nylon-jacketed line for your travel today."

"Nice," Morgan said. "I want one."

"I need to secure this side, and then we can zip line across." Hale frowned. "We'll have to leave the horses. You'll only be able to take what you can carry."

"That's fine." Dec slapped Hale on the shoulder. "Nice work."

Suddenly, there was a buzzing sound. Dec yanked out his satellite phone and looked at the screen. "Got some coverage. There's a message from Darcy." Then he cursed.

Logan felt his gut harden. "What?"

"Piero Costa was found dead today in Leymebamba."

Shit. Logan froze. "If the guide is dead, who the hell is with Sydney?" *Godammit*, he wanted to punch another tree.

"Looks like Silk Road got the drop on us." Dec shook his head, a muscle ticking in his jaw. "They somehow managed to replace the guide with one of their men."

"Come on." Logan yanked his backpack off his horse, stuffing some extra things inside. "We need to get moving and catch up to them." He pulled the pack on. "I'm going first."

Hale handed him a metal device with two rubber-gripped handles. "Here's the zip line trolley.

Slip it over the line and hold on. Good luck."

Logan moved to the edge of the cliff and fitted the trolley to the line. He tested it. It felt secure enough. He didn't care. He was going after Sydney, one way or another.

Logan gripped the handles and stepped off into air.

His weight hung down beneath the wire, and he whizzed across, picking up speed. He wasn't an adrenaline junkie like Callum, who was always climbing or racing something, but even Logan had to admit, this was damn fun. He looked down and saw the flowing water of the river below. Glancing up, he saw the rock face racing up to meet him.

He lifted his boots in front of him. He slammed into the rock, absorbing the impact with his knees.

Releasing one handle, he reached for the rocky edge and pulled himself out of the gorge. Gripping the trolley, he pressed the retract option, and it zipped back across the line.

Logan watched as the others came across. Declan, focused and intense. Morgan with a huge grin on her face. And Hale with an excited whoop.

Soon, they were all standing shoulder to shoulder, staring at the wall of overgrown forest, and the narrow dirt trail disappearing into it.

"This bastard who has Sydney has a good lead on us," Logan said darkly.

"We'll catch them," Dec said.

Yeah, they would. Sure, they were going to have to run up here at altitude with thin mountain air. But Logan was a former SEAL. This was nothing.

And he had two other ex-SEALs and one badass woman who could've been a SEAL if they'd let her. They could run all day and all night if they had to.

But he knew Morgan was the fastest of all of them.

"Morgan." He turned to his friend. "Can you run ahead and catch up? Stay close and make sure this bastard doesn't hurt her."

Morgan clasped his arm. "Sure thing."

A tiny bit of the tension in Logan eased.

Dec blew out a breath. "Okay, but Morgan, don't engage if you don't have to. Only step in if Sydney's in danger."

Morgan checked her handgun and nodded. She handed her backpack over to Logan. "See you soon. Don't dawdle, ladies."

"We'll catch you as soon as we can." Logan hitched up his and Morgan's backpacks and watched Morgan break into a run. The forest swallowed her long form. "Let's move."

***

Morgan Kincaid lengthened her stride and pushed for more speed.

The track was fine in places and a total mess in others. She pulled in deep breaths. And the air was thin. Still, she trained at altitude in Denver and the Rocky Mountains. This wasn't so bad.

She calculated she'd catch up with Sydney and the guy who'd taken her soon. The others couldn't be more than an hour behind her.

God, Logan was twisted up over this woman. Morgan had seen the way her friend watched Sydney Granger. She'd never seen him look at anyone like that.

Well, Morgan wasn't so sure that the slender, elegant Sydney was the right match for her friend. Logan needed someone who enjoyed the same things he did, who'd go his speed, and who'd love the brooding lug for himself.

Morgan frowned at the forest. She knew all about finding the wrong person. She dated. A lot. A whole, endless row of first dates. They always ended in disappointment.

She leaped over a rough patch of ground and spotted some creature scuttling into the bushes. She couldn't seem to find a man who could keep up with her: physically, sexually, emotionally. Hell, she couldn't find a man who even wanted to try.

Suddenly, she heard faint voices ahead. She slowed to a stop, trying to make out the words. She shook her head. Still too far away. She ducked into the thick vegetation.

Time for a little stealth.

She pulled out her Glock 22. Her man troubles were the least of her problems right now. In fact, she'd decided she was better off without a man.

And whatever Sydney Granger felt for Logan didn't matter. Logan had asked Morgan to take care of the woman.

Morgan had no intention of letting her friend down.

***

They'd been going for hours. Sydney barely noticed her tired and aching muscles. What she felt inside was far worse.

She closed her eyes. Logan and the others must be halfway back to Leymebamba by now. She felt the prick of tears in her eyes, but she blinked them back. Tears wouldn't help. She needed to focus, and wait for the opportunity to escape from fake Piero.

Then, she'd worry about Drew and her next step.

One thing she did know—she wasn't leading Silk Road to her brother.

At least her captor had removed the explosive device he'd put in her shirt. She was damn glad to have the thing gone. She hadn't gotten a good look at it, so she wasn't sure if it had been real or not, but she certainly wasn't taking any chances.

"Two more hours and we should reach the lake," fake Piero said with a grin. "We'll spend the night there in the tourist huts, and then my associates will meet us there in the morning."

Sydney's stomach did a slow roll. If Silk Road got her, they'd force her to find Drew. And if she refused, they'd kill her.

She swallowed, eyeing Piero. She *had* to escape from him.

She could do this. She had training he was unaware of, so with the element of surprise, she had a chance. She studied the surrounding forest, but she really didn't have a lot of options. She heard something heavy moving in the trees, out of view. *God, please don't be a jaguar.* That was all she needed.

Her mind whirled as she thought of ideas and discarded them. First, she needed to get him to stop, then she'd make a move.

But she'd only get one chance. Without the element of surprise, he'd overpower her.

She saw a length of decorative rope threaded on her horse's saddle. She slid her hand down and tugged on it. It pulled loose, and she coiled it in her hands. She tested the strength of it.

It would do the job.

"I need a break. My legs." She rubbed her thigh, feigning pain. They did hurt, but not that badly.

He muttered under his breath and then jerked his head. He stopped his horse and Sydney did the same. She slid off, leaning against the animal like she could barely stand.

"Water?" she asked.

With another bad-tempered mutter, he strode toward her, water bottle in hand.

Her hand tightened on the rope, dropping it down along her left leg.

He shoved the water bottle at her, and she took it with her right hand. As soon as he'd turned away, she dropped the water bottle to the ground and grabbed the other end of the rope. She took two steps, flung the loop of rope over his head, and pulled back hard against his throat.

He made a furious noise, his hands reaching up. His fingers scrabbled against his neck, trying to pull the rope away from his skin.

Sydney kicked at his knee. It was awkward from this angle, but his knee went out from under him and he fell into the dirt with a choked cry.

She strained backward, pulling on the rope. He slammed an elbow back, catching her in the belly. She gritted her teeth and held on.

Pass out, God damn you.

He was trying to turn around, and he wasn't losing consciousness. Fear spiked. *Dammit.*

A gunshot rang out, echoing in the trees.

Sydney fell backward with a cry and ducked. Another shot, and the horses started, letting out frightened whinnies.

She looked up.

Four armed figures emerged from the trees, weapons up.

A tall, broad man was in the lead. Air rushed into her lungs. *Logan.*

He charged past her, moving in and kicking the struggling fake Piero until he fell flat on his face.

"On your stomach, hands behind your head." The blunt words were delivered in a lethal tone that sent a chill through Sydney.

Logan grabbed the Silk Road man, yanking him to his feet. He patted him down, tossing a handgun to Hale. Then Logan shook the man viciously.

Sydney pushed up to sit. She saw Hale and Morgan calming the horses, and Declan striding forward.

"Logan," Declan said. "That's enough. We need to question him."

Logan dropped the man and he fell in a pile on

the ground. Declan stepped forward, zip ties in hand, and wrenched the man's wrists together behind his back. The Silk Road man cursed and struggled against his bonds.

Then her view of him was blocked by Logan's broad form. He knelt in front of her, staring into her face. "Did he hurt you?"

She looked into those fierce lion eyes and shook her head. What must he be thinking? What she'd said to him back at the bridge...he had to hate her.

"Logan..." When he just kept staring, she cleared her throat. "He had a small explosive, he put it on me back at the bridge."

Logan went still. Scary still. "He had an explosive on you."

She swallowed and saw fake Piero's eyes go wide.

"Don't let him near me," the Silk Road man spat out.

"Morgan." Declan jerked his head toward the horses. "You and Hale check for an explosive."

Sydney swallowed again. She felt like she had a rock in her throat. "Logan, I'm sorry. I was so afraid he'd hurt you and the others. I did what he told me to do, and I'm sorry."

Logan's brow creased. "You were trying to protect me?"

"Is that so hard to believe? I really am sorry about what I said."

Logan muttered a curse and then yanked her into his arms. He tugged her head back and his mouth touched hers. Sydney leaned into the kiss, a small sound escaping her.

His lips cruised across her cheek. "I see you, Sydney. The real you. I knew you were lying, and I knew something was wrong."

The heavy weight in her chest lifted, and something else rushed in, filling the space. Behind them, she heard Declan and the others talking about disposing of the explosive device. "Logan?"

"Yeah."

"Will you kiss me again?"

He pulled her back, his lips taking hers. The kiss was hot and hungry. His hands slid over her body, a firm, bold claim. She greedily kissed him back, the taste of him flooding her.

Sydney stopped thinking and just lost herself in Logan.

Chapter Nine

Logan took his time kissing Sydney. She was back in his arms and safe.

The sound of a clearing throat interrupted. Very reluctantly, Logan lifted his head and glared at Declan. His friend was grinning down at him.

Pulling Sydney closer, Logan absorbed the feel of her, liking when she snuggled into him. She fit perfectly in his arms.

"I want you guys to continue on to the lake," Dec said. "I'm going to stay here with our...friend. I have a few questions for him."

"And then what will you do with him?" Sydney asked.

Dec shrugged. "Tie him to a tree and leave him for the jaguars."

"Kill him," Logan added.

He saw the Silk Road man's eyes go wide, and he struggled against his ties. Logan let the bastard see that he was very serious.

Dec stepped in front of the man, blocking Logan's view. "Get Sydney to the lake. Find the cabins, and I'll catch up as soon as I can."

Sydney leaned forward. "He said other Silk Road

members would meet us at the lake. In the morning."

Dec's face hardened. "Good."

"I'll stay with Declan," Morgan said.

Hale rolled his eyes. "Great. I get to be the third wheel."

Logan grabbed Sydney's hand and pulled her up. "Come on, let's get moving." He grabbed the lead of her horse, and with Hale leading the other animal, they headed off down the track.

"You sure you're okay?" he asked her.

A faint smile. "Yes."

She was so damn beautiful. Logan had never really cared too much what a woman's face looked like. He'd always been a legs and breasts man. And while he had no trouble looking at Sydney's long legs, and high, firm breasts, he could look at her face all day.

Jeez, soon he'd start spouting poetry. He'd never been a hand-holder either, but here he was, with her slender fingers tangled with his. And he liked it.

"Logan, I really am sorry—"

He pulled her to a stop. "Don't be. You did what you had to do. You survived." He knew her work with the CIA hadn't fully prepared her for this kind of situation. Slowly, he lowered his head, and kissed her again.

Whistling cheerfully, Hale walked past them.

"Tonight—" Logan whispered "—you're mine."

He saw a flicker of something move in her eyes.

They kept trekking through the forest. He could

see she was starting to tire, and finally Logan suggested she ride the horse again. It felt like the forest was getting thicker, closing in around them.

"We should be getting close," Hale called back.

Logan hoped so. About twenty minutes later, Declan and Morgan jogged up behind them.

Dec slowed to a walk. "Our fake Piero confirmed that the rest of the Silk Road group he's working with are arriving tomorrow morning. His job was to keep Sydney captive until they arrived."

Logan barely resisted the urge to growl. "I don't trust him. We can't trust a word he says."

"Take it easy. I don't disagree, but I was fairly persuasive." Dec grinned. "I threatened to set you loose on him." Then Dec's face turned serious. "But I think we should set up a watch for tonight, just in case anyone tries to sneak up on us."

"I was hoping we'd get to see the ruins today," Sydney said.

Dec shook his head. "We won't have time. It'll be dark by the time we get there, and the chullpas are across the lake and up a steep cliff. There are some rustic cabins there that are used by the tourists. We'll get some rest, and then tomorrow, we'll explore the lake ruins."

"After we take down Silk Road," Logan added. Let the bastards come, he'd be ready for them.

"Even if you defeat them, more will come." Sydney's voice was harsh. "Silk Road seems unstoppable. You cut off a limb, but it grows right back."

"It won't grow back if you cut off its head," Logan said darkly.

"I don't think the Silk Road bosses are out here to do the dirty work," Declan said. "Hell, we don't even know who runs the damn group. Silk Road is seriously becoming a thorn in our side."

"I'll do whatever it takes to find my brother," Sydney said. "And then I'll do whatever I can to expose Silk Road to the world. They like the shadows, so I think it's time to shine some light on them."

Dec smiled. "I like you, Sydney."

Logan felt something ugly burn in his gut. He heard the admiration in Dec's voice. Declan was handsome, and far smoother than Logan. And before he'd fallen for Layne, he'd been popular with the ladies. Logan touched Sydney's arm. "You have your own woman."

Dec held up his hands. "So I do. And my friend, so do you. Doesn't mean I can't admire someone who is so beautiful and smart."

As his friend's words hit home, Logan waited for that feeling of acid that Annika had left in him. The panic at the thought of a woman belonging to him.

Nothing. Just a savage satisfaction and desire that was growing with every step.

His hand tightened on Sydney's.

He had to have her.

Soon.

***

Feeling tired and beat up, Sydney couldn't believe her eyes when they stepped out of the forest and crested a hilltop.

They all stopped.

Nestled like a dark jewel between steep hills was Laguna de los Condores.

The tangled forest vegetation grew right down to the lakeside, and, across it, in the dying light of day, she could see cliff faces. She strained to see if she could make out the burial chullpas, but too many shadows filled the view. She couldn't spot them.

Her gaze fell to the dark waters of the lake. It was so still, so quiet. She took a deep breath. After the action and adventure of the day, the calm peace of the place was amazing. It almost felt mystical. She could understand why the Warriors of the Clouds had chosen to bury their dead here.

"There are the huts," Morgan said, pointing.

Nearby, nestled on the side of the hill, were three very basic structures. Made of wood logs, and in a simple square shape, rustic was a generous label for them.

Hale took the leads of both horses. "I'll get these guys sorted out for the evening."

"Look at you go, cowboy," Morgan said.

Hale made a rude noise.

"Hide them," Declan said. "If Silk Road turns up unexpectedly, we don't want to announce our presence." He spun, with his hands on his hips, studying the area. "And no fire. We'll have to eat the MREs we brought with us."

Sydney watched them all move into action—checking out the huts, talking about defensive options, handing out the ready-to-eat meals, and determining the safest way down to the lake. They were such a tight group. A family.

It suddenly made her feel very alone. She loved Drew, but they didn't spend a lot of time together. She had good friends back in D.C., but they didn't anticipate each other like Declan and Logan did. She didn't have anyone who teased her, offered advice, and bumped their shoulder into hers like this group did.

Logan walked toward her and the tension in her eased. The look in his eyes told her that, at least for now, she wasn't alone.

Anticipation licked through her. This big, tough man wanted her. She'd kissed him, tasted him, and had his big cock in her hand. Oh, it was so easy to imagine how it would feel inside her, stretching her.

As darkness deepened, the shadows were growing, and she knew it was going to be incredibly dark through the night. Everyone dropped their backpacks in their designated huts, and soon they all sat together in Declan's. Inside, each hut was virtually bare, with a dirt-packed floor and some simple beds made of wooden frames and canvas.

Sydney listened as the THS team fought over the watch schedule for the night. Logan had the first few hours and Hale was putting up a fight about having the early morning. She munched on her bland meal. She was tired and hungry enough that it really didn't taste too bad.

"Okay, Hale, you're with me," Declan said, nodding at some empty plastic buckets they'd found in the huts. "We're going to head down to the lake and bring some water back."

Hale groaned, but followed his boss.

Logan walked Sydney to her hut next door. In the doorway, he tucked a strand of her hair back behind her ear. "Get into bed and get some rest."

She nodded, stepping inside. He'd pushed two of the simple beds together, unzipped their sleeping bags, and had them laid out on top.

"And make sure you're naked."

She froze. Desire was a rapid one-two punch to her belly.

Logan didn't move from the doorway. He didn't say anything else, just stared at her for a long, humming second, then stepped back. He disappeared out the door and into the darkness.

Sydney shivered and untied her hair. She pulled her boots off and set about untangling her hair.

Not long later, Declan brought her a bucket of water and said good night.

She pulled a cloth out of her backpack, stripped her clothes off, and washed up as best she could. Despite the cool air, the cold water felt great on her skin. She wiped the grime of the day away. As she moved the cloth over her belly, her breasts, her thighs, she felt a little trail of goosebumps. And a shimmer of arousal.

Closing her eyes, she imagined Logan skimming the damp cloth over her skin. The last time she'd had sex, her lover had taken her to an art gallery opening, followed by dinner at a restaurant with a three-month waiting list, and then they'd ended the night in a suite at one of D.C.'s fanciest hotels. And despite the extravagant build-up, the night had ended with more of a whimper than a bang.

Sydney opened her eyes and looked around the rustic hut. She grinned. Apparently the location and ambience didn't matter so much, since she'd never felt such desire for a man. She was trembling with anticipation, hungry for Logan's touch.

She climbed onto the bed and slid naked under the shiny fabric of the sleeping bag, certain she'd stay awake until he got back.

But as she stretched out, thinking about Logan, the strain and exertion of the day dragged her into sleep.

***

When Sydney woke, she wasn't sure where she was.

It was dark, but there was a low glow of light from a small lantern resting on the dirt floor. She blinked, as memories came rushing back. Laguna de los Condores.

The cobwebs of sleep disappeared.

She was lying on her belly, and suddenly very aware of the lips trailing down her back.

Logan kissed each knob of her spine, his rough hands kneading her back. She moaned. It felt so good. Without a word, he kept touching, stroking, and caressing her skin. He pressed his fingers deep into her sore muscles. He moved lower, reaching her buttocks and thighs. The man had very talented hands. She moaned again—it was so, so good.

He pressed his mouth to the top of her bottom, then cruised down one cheek. She writhed against the sleeping bag and looked back over her shoulder. A gasp escaped her. Logan looked rough and wild, desire etched starkly on his shadowed face. He lowered his head again, sprinkling kisses across the skin at the back of her thighs. When he nipped gently, she felt a rush of dampness between her legs.

As his lips moved closer to where she wanted them, she squirmed. His palms kneaded the globes of her ass and his mouth nipped her again.

"Logan."

He gripped her hips and urged her up on her hands and knees. She barely even noticed the cool night air on her skin—she was completely focused on Logan. She heard him make a hungry sound and he parted her with his fingers. Then his mouth was on her, moving between her legs.

Sydney jerked and cried out. His tongue lapped at her, all of it firm, ruthless strokes. He licked and sucked, his tongue stabbing inside her. She gripped the fabric beneath her in her hands, his name spilling from her lips.

He pushed her legs wider apart. "Come for me, Sydney." A deep growl.

He kept eating at her, pulling her deeper. Then

she felt his lips close over her clit. One hard suck, and she exploded.

Still shuddering, pleasure coursing through her, she felt him spin her around. He lifted and moved her so easily with his strong arms. Her back pressed to the bed and he kneeled over her, his hard, uncut cock standing up toward his hard abs. She saw him reach out and then heard the crinkle of a wrapper. Licking her lips, she watched him slide the condom over his cock.

Then he gripped her legs, pushing them apart.

He stroked her. "So swollen and plump. Just for me."

Circling his cock with one hand, he leaned forward and rubbed the head between her legs. She gasped.

"You'll feel this, Sydney. Every inch."

"Yes, Logan. Come inside me."

"I'm going to make you mine."

She let her gaze run over him. His rugged face. The scars across his chest. His wide shoulders. He pushed one of her legs up, and his gaze locked with hers as the thick head of his cock slid between her folds.

Her breathing sped up, turning irregular. *Oh, God.* She felt a pleasurable stretch as he filled her.

"Take me, Sydney."

"I'm trying," she gasped out.

With a hard push, he thrust inside her.

A cry escaped her. He was so big, stretching her hard. He was so overwhelming. She forced herself to relax, and then she felt his rough hands sliding down her leg. She stretched her arms above her head, arching into him.

"Sydney...damn, you feel good." His voice was strained.

His thrusts started slowly at first—firm and to the hilt. Then he gained momentum until he was slamming into her. He changed the angle of his thrusts and she felt him pressing against her clit. She wrapped her legs around his hips. The dizzying rush of sensation left Sydney lightheaded.

"That's it. Damn, you're tight."

Logan pulled out and slammed back in. Sydney moaned, her eyes widening. He was so big, so forceful, so much. She felt like he was claiming every inch of her.

As he hammered into her, faster and faster, sweat sheened his chest and his muscles were straining.

"I want you to come again, Sydney. This time with my cock deep inside you." His words ended with a fierce growl.

***

Logan continued to drive into Sydney. So tight. So hot. So sweet. He was barely holding back his own release.

Looking down, he watched her make sexy little noises, her lovely breasts moving with each of his thrusts. The scent of her arousal swamped him, driving him to the edge. He wanted to watch her come again. He continued to drive into her, keeping his gaze locked on hers.

Then she gasped, her body tightening around him, clamping down hard. She threw her head back.

A second later, his release slammed into him like a blast. He groaned, his back bowing, his fingers digging into her skin.

He collapsed, chest heaving. He moved to the side and pulled her limp, warm body close. Her eyes were closed, her chest rising and falling in shallow breaths.

Logan tightened his hold on her for a second, then reluctantly he let go and stood. It only took him a second to discard the condom. And as he turned back and took in the slender limbs, the pretty breasts, and the fall of her blonde hair spread out around her beautiful face, he felt need flaring to life again already. *Hell*.

He climbed back into the bed, and pulled her close. Burying his face in her hair, he breathed her in. She turned and curled into him.

When was the last time he cuddled in bed with a woman? *Never*. Not even in his short-lived, disastrous tangle with Annika.

He slid a hand down Sydney's body, lazily stroking her smooth skin.

Then she moved, pushing up, and studying the backs of his arms. Her fingers traced over his tattoos.

"I really like these," she said. "They suit you."

He let her push him until he was lying on his stomach, his head pillowed on his arms. She moved, her hands tracing down his back, over his wolf tattoo. The look on her face as she explored him... He'd never had a woman look at him like that before. He'd definitely not had a woman like Sydney Granger stare at his tattoos the same way he guessed she'd look at some piece of fancy art in a gallery.

He sat up, pulling her into his lap, her back pressed to his chest. He cupped her breasts. "I really like these. They suit you."

She laughed. But as he gently tugged at her nipples, her laughter gave way to a ragged breath. She moved against him, her sweet, rounded butt grinding against him. Of course, she felt his now-hard-again cock.

She arched her head back. "You're ready again?"

"I've got good stamina."

Her laugh was low and throaty.

Then he stilled. "But I only had one condom."

She matched his stillness and cleared her throat. "I'm on birth control. And I'm healthy."

He knew her measured words meant that she didn't usually do this kind of thing. The trust she was putting in him made his chest warm.

His hands flexed on her skin. The thought of sliding inside her without any barrier, without a layer of latex between them...

"I had a checkup two weeks ago," he said. "I'm clean."

Her smile was slow and sexy. "Well, then, Wild Man, show me what else you've got."

He forced her head back and took her mouth

with his. A second later, he rolled, pulled her beneath him and slid home.

Chapter Ten

Sydney made a humming noise of pleasure.

She was on her knees, her hands digging hard into Logan's strong thighs, taking his big cock in her mouth.

He groaned. God, she loved this. Seeing the effect she had on him. The musky taste of him.

His hand slid into her hair, his grip hard enough to sting. "You like that, don't you?" he said between gritted teeth.

She pulled back, running her tongue over the head of him. She saw the strong muscles of his stomach go tight. "I like giving you pleasure."

"You like the control."

She smiled. "That, too." She swallowed him back into her mouth.

He let her move on him a few more times, then his hands slid under her arms.

"Enough." He yanked her up, spun her, and pressed her down against the edge of the bed.

Her knees hit the sleeping bag she'd been kneeling on before, the edge of the bed pressing against her belly. His big body covered her from behind, the hair on his thighs tickling the back of hers. A second later, his cock thrust inside her without warning.

Her moan was long and loud. He pulled out and thrust back inside. He was so deep, and she was so full.

He showed her no mercy. Logan wasn't a smooth or easy lover. He was rough and wild, and she loved every minute of it.

He possessed her, keeping up his hard, firm strokes. She felt his callused fingers sliding under her, tracing down her belly. He found her clit.

"Yes, Logan."

A few hard flicks and the pleasure coalesced into a hard ball in her belly, then exploded. As she shuddered under the pleasure, he ground inside her and held himself there, growling as he spilled inside her.

They both stayed there, bent over the edge of the bed, breathing heavily.

"Hell of a way to wake up." His voice was husky. He pulled back and pressed a kiss to her shoulder blade. "The best damn way."

She felt the same. She'd never felt this close to any man before.

As he pulled out of her, she let out a little moan. "I really hope we don't have to ride any horses today." She was more than a little sore between her thighs.

He pressed another kiss to the back of her neck and then stood. As he walked over to the bucket of water, she managed to collapse on the bed. She watched him as he splashed water onto himself. It ran down his chest and he washed himself with quick, easy swipes—chest, underarms, genitals. Sydney leaned back on the bed, wishing they had a hot shower and she could be running soapy hands over his intriguing cock and balls. He dressed with quick, economical movements and she hated seeing him cover his muscles and tattoos.

"The sun will be up soon," he said. "We'll head across the lake and take a look at the burial sites. See what your brother's left for you."

Their interlude was over. She felt the rude sting of harsh reality creeping back in. For one night, for those long, hot hours, she'd been able to forget about the people after her and her brother. "And Silk Road?"

"We'll see them coming. Dec's got a few things planned."

"Unless they ran into fake Piero and he told them everything."

Logan's face turned dark. "Hopefully a jaguar found him first." He finished doing up his shirt, his gaze running over her. "I'll get some fresh water from the lake." He grabbed the bucket and headed outside.

Sydney worked on untangling her hair and preparing herself for the day. She hoped—prayed— they found Drew today.

Logan was back soon with the bucket. He set it down and strode over to the bed. He reached down, cupped her breast, then stroked down her belly. His touch was filled with an easy, possessive claim, like he had every right. Like her body was all his.

She felt her pulse spike. "Go," she said. "Or we'll end up naked again."

"That's not really a deterrent, babe."

"Go." She made a shooing motion with her hand.

He leaned down, pressed a long, deep kiss to her mouth, then he was gone.

Sydney took her time. She washed up, running the cloth over her body. She cruised it over each bruise, each patch of whisker burn, and the pleasant ache between her legs. She smiled to herself. Big, wild Logan was all hers.

It didn't take her long to dress. She stuffed all the other items back in her backpack and Logan's. She glanced around the hut. The simple beds. The dirt floor. She was almost sorry to leave.

She hitched her bag over her shoulder and strode out into the morning air. The sun was coming up, the faint blush of dawn coloring the forest. There was a hush over the lake and the trees. It was so beautiful.

She spotted the THS team nearby, huddled tightly and talking quietly. She joined them.

"Any sign of Silk Road?"

Logan shook his head. "Nothing."

Declan pointed to an overgrown path down to the lake. "There are four small, wooden boats at the edge of the lake. We'll head across the water and take all the boats with us. If Silk Road heads this way, we'll see them from the other side, and they'll have no easy way to get across the lake."

They made the steep trek down to the water. The trees ran right to the edge in a wild tangle.

Sydney stared at the boats dubiously. They looked handmade and not in particularly good condition.

Hale, Morgan, and Declan each climbed into a boat and pushed off. Logan held the edge of the final boat and waved her in. She climbed in and Logan pushed them away from the edge and leaped in behind her. It rocked under his weight. He grabbed some oars and soon they were powering across the still waters of Laguna de los Condores.

"It must have looked exactly like this when the Warriors of the Clouds were here," she said. "It feels almost mystical out here on the water. It's so easy to see why they chose this place."

"Look." Logan lifted his chin toward the approaching cliff face.

She stared, not seeing what he was talking about. Then she spotted one of the chullpas nestled against the cliff under an overhang. Her heart sped up. It was high above the water.

Soon, the boat nudged up to the shore. Logan climbed out, secured the boat, and then helped her out.

Declan pulled out a machete, and they started the steep, muddy hike up to the chullpas. Sydney grabbed onto anything she could to keep her balance and to stop from slipping. Finally, they reached some rough, wooden ladders pressed into the side of the steep hill.

"Left by the archeologists," she said.

They climbed steadily. Sydney paused once to look back over the lake and surrounding forests. Stunning.

Soon, she reached the top and climbed up onto a ledge. Right in front of her was a chullpa. It was carved into the cliff face, and in places, she could see remnants of white, red, and yellow paint.

"Hale, keep watch," Declan murmured.

The other man nodded, pulling a set of binoculars from his backpack.

"Drew's notes said there are six surviving chullpas, and the remnants of one that didn't survive," Sydney said, stepping carefully as she moved closer to the chullpa. "They each housed mummies and offerings. The mummies were all wrapped in textiles and well-preserved."

She looked at the carved holes and ledges, imagining the funerary bundles that must have sat there for so many hundreds of years.

"Freaky," Morgan said.

Sydney turned and looked at a row of skulls and bones lined up on a rock ledge. "When the place was looted, some mummies were destroyed, as the looters looked for metal and jewelry. I guess the archeologists didn't take anything that wasn't intact." The empty eyes of the skulls looked out over the lake. "The offerings here were only ceramics, textiles, feathered headdresses. A shame the grave robbers destroyed so much."

And now Silk Road was looking to pillage the Warriors of the Clouds once again.

"So, was it the Chachapoyan bigwigs who were buried here?" Logan asked. He was staring at some of the artwork still visible on the stone walls.

"No one knows for sure. It seems that some of

the mummies didn't have the kind of wear and tear that life back then inflicted, which means they were probably elite. But the Cloud Warriors seemed pretty egalitarian, and mummies of people at all social levels have been found."

As she touched the stone where a mummy must have rested, she imagined Drew standing there, doing the same thing. What would he have done here? Where would he leave her a message?

In her mind's eye, she could picture her brother wandering around, snapping pictures, recording what he saw.

She turned and saw Logan and Declan looking back across the lake, alert and tense. Hale stood beside them looking through the binoculars.

"Any movement?" Declan asked.

"Nothing," Hale responded.

Sydney sat down near the row of skulls, looking out at their fabulous view. "I'm sorry your rest has been disturbed," she said quietly. She noticed one skull was turned, looking back at the chullpa. It reminded her of the time Drew had scared her at Halloween with a plastic skull. He'd left it beside her bed.

Her gaze narrowed on the skull. She rose, moving closer. The skull was looking at a crack in the stone.

And there was something wedged in the crack.

Her heart started thumping. It wasn't big, but whatever it was, didn't belong in a Cloud Warrior ruin. She reached in and pulled it out.

Sydney held up the memory card. "I think I

found what my brother left me."

***

Logan felt the excitement and hope radiating off Sydney. She handed the memory card over to Dec with a shaking hand.

But Logan's gaze was snagged on her face. He'd watched every flicker of emotion cross over her elegant features throughout the night.

It was the wildest, hottest night of his life. She'd not only kept up with him and his sexual demands, she'd not been afraid to demand her own pleasure. Under the classy, elegant exterior was a woman who knew what she liked and took what she wanted.

Whatever happened on this job, he'd decided he was keeping her.

Sydney was his.

Hell, he'd even drink her fancy wine and mushy cheese if he had to.

Dec slipped the memory card into his tablet and handed it to Sydney. She tapped the screen, and smiled. "There's a video recording."

A second later, Drew Granger's face filled the screen. "Sydney. God, I hope it's you watching this and that you're okay." Her brother released a long breath.

"He looks tired," she murmured, gripping the edges of the tablet.

Logan didn't know Drew Granger, but the young man did look exhausted.

"I never meant for this to happen," Drew continued. "I was having a blast researching the Chachapoyas. They are *such* a fascinating people. I believe they were even more advanced than history remembers. Their advanced surgeries, the advanced training of their warriors, their building techniques...and, Sydney, they were metalsmiths. They had gold, silver, and other metals." The man smiled. "I found reference to them hiding their treasure in a temple. They were fighting the Inca and they knew they couldn't hold out against the Incas' superior numbers. Like the Inca, the Cloud Warriors used knotted quipus to record their information. No one has ever decoded a quipu, they remain a complete puzzle." He grinned wildly. "But I did, Sydney! I decoded a Cloud Warrior quipu and discovered they moved their valuables deep into the forest. Gold, silver, jewelry, and best of all, records of their knowledge." He threw his hands out. "It'll be the biggest find of the century." Then he frowned. "But I messed up. I was celebrating in a bar in Lima and a beautiful woman...she seemed so interested in me and my work. I told her everything." He shook his head. "I'm such an idiot. I should've known a woman like her wouldn't really be interested in a geek like me."

Logan could guess what happened next. He felt for the man. Logan knew exactly what a betrayal like that felt like.

"They came after me the next day. I managed to get away." Drew sighed. "They call themselves Silk Road and they're dangerous. Really dangerous.

Sydney, I know they're coming after you to get to me. You have to be careful. I'm sorry, sis." A weak smile. "At least I know you can look after yourself."

Logan flexed his fingers. So Drew was happy to throw his sister to the wolves? Logan felt a muscle tick in his jaw. He'd have a few things to say to the man when they found him.

"I'm going after the treasure, Sydney." Now the man's smile was rueful. "This time I'll make it a little easier for you. No more games. My research shows they moved their treasure to one of their most remote cities. A place called Lapoc. I'm going there now. See you when you find me." The recording cut off.

"He's okay." Sydney smiled, then she muttered a curse. "I wish he'd just come home. Screw the treasure. It isn't worth his life. I just want him safe."

"Don't worry." Logan pressed a hand to the back of her neck and squeezed. "We're going to find him."

***

"All right, I'm going to try and contact Darcy," Declan said.

Nodding, Sydney handed back the tablet.

Declan used his satellite connection. "If anyone can work out the location of this city of Lapoc, it's Darcy." He shot a look at Hale. "Any sign of our friends?"

Hale lowered his binoculars. "Still nothing. Doesn't feel right."

Sydney watched Logan and the others scan the far side of the lake. They were all tense, Logan most of all, and she could tell that he didn't like it either.

"Where the hell are they?" Logan said.

"Maybe Piero lied?" Sydney suggested.

Logan's scowl said he wasn't buying it.

"Connection's going through." Declan held up the tablet.

Darcy's face filled the screen, but the connection was bad and her image flickered.

"Hey, Darce, we made it to the lake," Declan said. "We had a little trouble along the way."

Darcy leaned forward. "Let me guess. First word starts with S and second word starts with R."

"We took care of it, but we know more Silk Road members are on the way here. We found another clue from Drew Granger. What can you find out about the location of a place called Lapoc?"

Darcy tapped the keyboard. "What is it?"

"A remote jungle city of the Cloud Warriors, according to Granger."

Darcy shook her head, her hair brushing her jaw. "There's no record of a Lapoc in connection with the Cloud People." She frowned. "No mention of it at all."

They all fell silent. Sydney felt her stomach fall to her feet. "That can't be. My brother definitely said Lapoc, and he said no more games—" Sydney broke off.

"What?" Logan asked.

"Another silly game from when we were kids. He'd always say 'no more games' to lull me into a false sense of security, then fool me one more time."

Logan stroked his stubbled cheeks. "So Lapoc isn't really the location?"

Sydney ran a hand through her hair. "I'm not sure. Darcy, can you run combinations of the letters in the name. See if something pops up? It was another thing Drew always liked to do. Anagrams of letters."

Darcy nodded. "It might take a little while—" A beep came through the connection "—or not. Not much is known about the Chachapoya language, but it is theorized that *lap* means fortress. It's added to the end of place names."

"Like the Kuelap ruins," Sydney said.

"Right. *Oc* isn't so clear cut. It is speculated it means puma or bear, or maybe jaguar."

Sydney straightened. "So not *Lapoc*, it should be *Oclap*. Fortress of the Jaguar."

"I've found a very vague reference to the ruins of a remote city that was found in dense, overgrown forest not too far from your location. It showed characteristics of Chachapoya cities—large defensive walls, ruins of circular buildings. But that was years ago, and no one's been back to investigate it. It's about a five-hour trek from Laguna de los Condores."

"That must be it. Thanks, Darcy," Declan said. "Can you send the info through to me?"

"Already done. Declan, you guys stay safe."

"Always try to," Declan answered. "Tell Layne I said hi."

"Will do." Darcy blinked off.

"Plan?" Logan asked.

A map flashed on the screen. The lake was clear, as was the glowing yellow dot to the south-east of the lake.

"We trek to the location." Declan touched the dot. "We're looking for any sign of Drew Granger."

"And the treasure?" Morgan asked.

"Not our priority. If we find it, we'll note the location, and I'll ensure the Peruvian government knows about it."

Sydney wasn't so sure Drew would give the treasure up so easily. But Declan was right, finding Drew was the only thing that mattered.

"Dec!" Hale's urgent voice. The big man spun to face them. "I'm sure I saw movement in the trees. Very stealthy."

"Jaguar?"

"I don't think so."

Declan was frowning. "By the huts?"

"No. *This* side of the lake. Just south of our location."

Declan and Logan cursed. Sydney felt them all stiffen. She turned and scanned the trees.

She didn't see anything.

Then she smelled something. With a frown, she took a deep breath. *Oh, no.*

"I smell smoke." Her gaze met Logan's. "Fire!"

Chapter Eleven

Down the hill, Logan saw the flames licking up the trees.

Declan spun and shoved the tablet into Logan's hand. "Logan, take Sydney and get to the ruins."

"This is a trap, Dec. They want us to run—"

"That's why Hale, Morgan, and I will hold them off and give you a chance to get away."

The flames were growing, the crackling sound of it becoming louder. Then he heard a very familiar sound. Gunfire.

Bullets slammed into the trees behind them.

Fuck. He ducked for cover, wrapping one arm around Sydney and taking her with him.

Dec crouched beside them. "Keep going up. We can't go back down the ladder."

Logan felt torn. He hated to leave his friends to face these bastards alone. But a part of him wanted to get Sydney to safety. Hell of a choice. His friends or his woman.

Dec made the decision for him. "Go." Dec clasped Logan's hand. "We'll catch up. I promise."

And his friend had never broken a promise to Logan. He'd been stupid to trust Annika, but his trust in Dec had never been wrong. Nor his trust in the woman pressed to his side, watching him with faith on her face.

"Don't get shot," Logan growled. "Layne will be pissed if you do. She wasn't that pleased the last time it happened."

A faint smile from Dec. "You got it. Now *go.*"

Logan tossed Hale and Morgan a quick salute and grabbed Sydney's hand. He pulled her along the ledge and into the trees. Shifting his grip on his machete, he started hacking a way up the steep slope.

Smoke thickened around them. Sydney started coughing. Logan pulled his outer shirt off and tore strips off the bottom. "Here." He tied it over her mouth and then did the same for himself. "Now, we need to move fast—" his words were muffled by the cloth "—and put as much distance between them and us as we can." He pulled the tablet up to check the map again, looked up at the sun, and then he set off.

They pushed as hard as they could through the thick trees. At times, it was really hard going, and they slipped on the steep, muddy ground. Finally, they crested the hill...and moved into even thicker forest.

Here, there were no tracks to follow. Logan had to hack away vines and undergrowth to make a way through.

Soon, the smoke cleared, and the noises from the lake were gone—no gunfire or shouting. Dec and the others would be okay. Logan knew they were all tough and they never gave up. They could take care of the Silk Road mercenaries with their hands tied behind their backs. Hell, he was sure Morgan could take care of them all on her own.

Logan focused on getting Sydney to Oclap.

They'd been going hard for an hour, when Sydney stumbled to a stop. "Need to...rest." She was breathing hard.

He nodded, lowering the machete. "Here." He handed her a water bottle. "You doing okay?"

She nodded. "Just give me a minute and I'll be fine." She lifted the bottle and chugged some water back. She was sweating, her hair sticking to her temples. "I can't believe what Silk Road are willing to do for this treasure. Kill, burn down the forest, possibly destroy those burial chullpas back there..."

"Money. Power. Greed. It's the same story over and over again."

Sydney tilted her head. "You're thinking about that female agent again."

"Yeah." But funnily enough, the acid burn in his gut didn't feel quite so bad anymore.

Sydney screwed the lid back on the bottle, and handed it back to him. "Let's go find my brother, and make sure Silk Road does *not* get its hands on a single piece of the Cloud Warrior treasure."

Logan smiled at her. "I like it when you get all forceful and bossy."

She slapped a hand against his chest. "That was nothing. Later, I'll show you forceful and bossy."

They started moving again.

Logan pushed her hard. She kept moving and she didn't complain, keeping up with his pace.

After two more hours, he pulled up. "Let's take a break."

She nodded, leaning against a tree. He couldn't ask for a better partner to trek with. She was smart and tough. Beautiful and sexy. And his. Logan felt something unfamiliar shift inside him. Shit. *Shit.*

She looked up and smiled at him. Those boiling emotions inside him morphed into something else. They'd once again escaped a dangerous situation, could have been killed. There were several hours between them and danger...but he wouldn't be happy until she was one hundred percent safe and far away from Silk Road.

He felt a primitive need to claim her, to mark this woman as his.

He took a step toward her. Her eyes widened. He wanted her. Now. He yanked her to him, and slammed his mouth over hers. The kiss was wild and out-of-control. Soon, she was making tiny noises, trying to climb up his body. Without stopping to think, he tore her trousers open and pushed them down.

"Logan," she gasped.

He had her pinned up against the trunk of the tree. He opened his own trousers, and freed his cock. He curled his hand around her ass, cupping her buttocks, and pushed her up. She wrapped her legs around his hips.

A second later, he shoved inside her. She made a choked sound, her nails digging into his shoulders.

"You're so thick."

And she was so tight and wet. He started moving, pistoning inside her, trembling with the fury of his need. Her mouth found his ear, nipping and sucking, and she made hungry little sounds. Logan felt like a wild animal, driven only by the single need to claim her, mate with her.

She stiffened and cried out his name. Her body bowed in his arms, and she shook under the force of her orgasm.

As her body clenched down on his, he managed two more powerful thrusts before his release exploded inside her.

When it was over, only the tree was holding them both upright. Wrecked, Logan fought to clear his head and find some control.

God, he'd been rough with her. Remorse flooded him. He'd never been so rough with a woman before.

He pulled back, and his cock slid out of her. She made a small sound of protest, and he got a good look at her. Her cheeks were flushed, and in her eyes he saw…intense satisfaction and bliss.

He frowned. "You're okay?"

Her smile was a little crooked. "Better than okay."

"I was rough."

"And I liked it." Then she got a good look at his face and one of her silky brows rose. "Wild Man, I can handle anything and everything you've got."

He smiled back at her, cupping her cheek with his hand. Then he stepped back with a regretful sigh. "We need to keep moving. It was dumb of me to do this, but..."

"But?" she prompted.

"I couldn't help myself."

She smiled, tucking her shirt back into her trousers. "Then let's keep moving."

***

Another hour and a half of trekking left Sydney's body numb. Her legs were moving, but she didn't feel them anymore. Her muscles were so tired. She followed right behind Logan's broad form and secretly cursed his seemingly endless stamina. The man was a machine.

"We're getting close," he called back.

Every few minutes he kept looking back to check on her. It made her smile. Her big protector. He could explode into violence or passion in a flash. The deadly fighter one second, and generous lover or concerned protector the next.

And she was falling for him. Her feet stopped moving. *Oh, God.*

He looked back with a frown. "What's wrong?"

She cleared her throat and forced herself to move again. "Nothing."

"From the look on your face, it isn't nothing."

She kept walking. "I just realized something."

He was so close she could feel the heat coming off him. "What?"

"Drop it, Logan."

"No. If it makes you look like someone smacked you in the head, I want to know what it is."

Pushy alpha male. She stopped and shoved her hands on her hips. "Fine. I realized that despite your wild and sometimes antisocial ways, I think I'm falling in love with you."

He jerked to a halt and she watched his back tense. He turned, and for the first time since she'd met him, his eyes were as big as saucers.

Even though her heart hurt, Sydney let out a laugh. "I think you'd look less terrified if I said there was a platoon of Silk Road thugs behind you."

"I'm not terrified."

She tried not to let his lackluster response hurt her. But that look on his face did sting. A lot.

She shook her head. "Come on, we need to keep moving—"

He grabbed her arm, and reluctantly she looked up at him.

"I'm...glad."

She blinked. "What?"

"I'm glad. Because I've decided you're mine and I'm keeping you."

She didn't know whether to hit him or kiss him. "I'm not a chew toy, Logan."

He grinned. "I like chewing on you."

She cocked her head. "Why?"

"Why do I like chewing on you?"

She ignored that. "Why do you want to keep me?"

"Because." He turned, lifted his machete, and started to slash at the vegetation.

"That's not an answer, Logan."

He grunted.

"*This* is your way of talking about your feelings?"

"Men don't talk about feelings," he said in a bad-tempered tone.

She pushed some vines aside and snorted. "Right. You know who doesn't talk about their feelings? Cavemen."

Logan spun and grabbed the front of her shirt. He yanked her in close and she was forced up on her tiptoes.

"I'm not good at it, okay? I'm better at showing how I feel." He loosened his grip, his hand sliding up to circle her throat. He stroked her skin gently.

She softened, but she wasn't planning to let him off that easily. Then she noticed something behind him, through the holes in the vines he'd just hacked at.

"Logan, my God. Turn around."

He spun.

Together they stared at the giant stone walls rising up from the forest floor.

***

Logan led the way, walking along the base of the wall. He saw a snake slither away into the undergrowth and decided not to mention it to Sydney.

He was looking for some sort of entrance like they'd seen in the walls at Kuelap. Sure enough, they came to a narrow gap in the wall.

UNEXPLORED

"Here." Holding her hand, they walked through the portal.

"Wow," Sydney breathed. "Incredible."

Logan took in the ruined city. Yeah, it was incredible. In Cambodia, he'd seen a secret underground temple. In Egypt, the amazing ruins of a lost oasis.

This find was equally as amazing.

The ruins resembled the fortress of Kuelap. There were lots of ruined round houses, walls, terraces, and platforms. Here, the jungle had claimed the city, and much of it was overgrown.

Toward the far end of the city, he could see a huge stone platform. And in the center of it was a large, circular temple made of giant blocks of stone.

"Drew!" Sydney cupped her hands together and called out her brother's name.

Silence.

Logan saw her shoulders sag. "Come on, let's take a look around."

They wandered through the ancient stones. He imagined the warriors who'd lived here building the place, maintaining it, until they'd been driven from their home.

"Drew mentioned a temple." Sydney was staring up at the circular structure.

"We'll look everywhere."

The minutes ticked by as they moved through the ruins. With each empty building and crumbling ruin, he saw the worry on Sydney's face deepen.

It wasn't long before they reached the large platform and temple.

From the base, they stared up. The temple was built in a huge circle.

"Amazing," Sydney said. "I can imagine the Warriors of the Clouds moving up here to give thanks to their gods."

They climbed the stairs and stood in front of the doorway into the temple. Sydney peered inside.

It was then Logan noticed something on the ground. He stiffened. It was a puddle of blood. He crouched and touched it, rubbing his fingers together.

Fresh blood.

"What is it?" She came to his side.

He grabbed her hand, felt her freeze.

"Blood," she whispered.

"It may not be human." Then he spotted something else nearby.

A bloody handprint pressed against the ground.

"Looks like we didn't need your brother after all." The deep, faintly accented voice made them both spin.

Logan was reaching for his Desert Eagle, but the fake Piero was already aiming his gun at Sydney.

"Put the weapon down and kick it over here." The man gestured with his fingers. He had three other people behind them, all of them armed.

Anger vibrating through him, Logan did it. He should have damn well heard these guys coming. He dropped his gun to the dirt and kicked it across to the man. He eyed them all, assessing them. Ex-military, and they all looked tough and seasoned.

"Knew I should've killed you when I had the

chance." Molten anger ran through Logan's veins. He struggled to clamp it down and keep some control. He couldn't lose it right now. "How did you escape my team?"

"We set the fire, and I had enough people to keep them busy while I came after you and Ms. Granger." His smile was ugly. "Now. Let's find the treasure." He glared at Logan. "And later, I'm going to kick you in the ribs until I break them." He touched his side. "Like you did to me."

One of his people, a fit, athletic, blonde woman, moved forward and patted Logan down. She was tall, with broad shoulders, and a set face that warned everyone not to mess with her. She grabbed his machete and relieved him of his knife.

"Oh, and Mr. O'Connor?" Piero said. "If you step out of line, I shoot Ms. Granger in the head. Understand?"

"Yeah." Logan was going to rip this guy's head off when he got the chance.

Piero waved his team toward the temple. They walked through the narrow entrance. It was pitch-black inside, and Piero's people pulled out flashlights and turned them on.

Logan stayed close to Sydney. They moved through several empty rooms, and Logan realized the main tunnel was moving downward, into the ground. They passed beautiful artwork on the walls in the characteristic Chachapoya design.

"You two are going to help me score a promotion," Piero said, studying the walls. "My bosses have been less than impressed with losing out to Treasure Hunter Security."

A muscle ticked in Logan's jaw, but he stayed silent.

"Why do you do this?" Sydney asked. "Hurt people, kill people…all for treasure?"

Piero moved his flashlight and looked at her. "I wouldn't expect you to understand, Ms. Granger. You grew up in privilege, with money." A look crossed the man's face. "You have no idea what it's like to come from nothing, have nothing, be forced to do things you don't want to do."

"There are always choices," she said.

"No," the man answered, his tone void of emotion. "There aren't. Keep moving."

Finally, they came to a large room cut completely from stone. It was lined with ledges and cavities, similar to those they'd seen in the chullpas at the lake.

But these cavities were not filled with mummies.

These were filled with treasure.

The Silk Road team started laughing and joking, Piero turned in a circle as his team flashed their lights around.

Logan saw the glint of gold and silver. There were statues, jewelry, golden headdresses.

Sydney moved closer to the wall, and Logan followed. Inside one alcove were stacks of what look like string.

"Quipus," Sydney said. "This is how they recorded their information. There could be amazing things stored on here." She scowled at the Silk Road people, who were already starting to pull treasure off the shelves and stuff it into bags. "This is wrong. This treasure was hidden from the Inca, from the Spanish, from looters." There was anger vibrating in her voice.

Logan was more worried about the fact that he and Sydney were no longer required.

Their reason for being kept alive was gone.

Where the hell were Declan and the others?

"Sydney." Logan leaned in close and kept his voice very low. "We need to get out of here."

She nodded, eyeing Piero and his men. They took a few stealthy steps back toward the doorway.

At that moment, Piero turned. "Oh, you're ready to leave?" He raised his handgun. "I can help you with that."

"Go!" Logan shouted, pushing Sydney toward the doorway.

With gunshots reverberating around them, they ran into the tunnel.

Chapter Twelve

Without a flashlight, the exit tunnel was pitch dark. They were running blind and Sydney felt a burning pain tearing through her side. She stumbled.

"Keep going," Logan barked.

She pressed her hand to her side. She could feel sticky blood oozing through her fingers. Gritting her teeth, she ignored the pain and kept running. She didn't want to slow Logan down. Behind them, she could hear the Silk Road men shouting.

She focused on staying upright, and getting out of the dark temple.

A second later, they stumbled out of the temple and into the dappled forest sunshine.

Logan barely slowed down. He yanked her toward the stairs of the platform. "We need to get out of the walls and hide in the forest."

She bit her lip and started down the stairs. Every step was agony.

At the base of the steps, he turned. Then he looked down. His face turned gray. "Sydney."

She looked down. *Uh oh*. Her entire shirt was covered in blood.

She managed a weak smile. "I think I got shot."

Carefully, he pulled her behind the ruins of a nearby building. He nudged her down on a rock and lifted her shirt with shaking hands.

"Shit."

She couldn't look. "I'm fine. We need to go."

He tore his shirt off over his head, and wadded the fabric. He pressed it to her side. "Bullet's gone into your side."

Suddenly, voices and shouts broke out, coming from the direction of the temple. There was the sound of footsteps thundering on stone.

"Keep the pressure on." He helped her up and slid an arm around her. "We have to get out of here."

She nodded. She steeled herself and bit down on her lip to stop from crying out. They hobbled as fast as they could, back toward the entrance in the outer walls.

They stumbled down between the ruins of two round houses, when something moved ahead of them. They halted. A creature stepped out of the patchy shadows and leaped onto a block of stone.

Sydney gasped. A jaguar.

It was sleek and strong, the tan fur of its powerful body dotted with gorgeous black rosettes. It stared at them with a lazy arrogance.

"Dammit." Logan pulled her backward. "Just move slowly." They took several steps back, and then Logan pulled her to the left, behind a ruined wall. They set off in that direction.

"This leads us away from the entrance," she whispered.

"We'll circle back."

A gunshot. Logan ducked and yanked her to the right, pain exploding in her side. They crouched behind a low stone wall. Sydney sucked in air, panting, trying to fight off a wave of dizziness. The pain was excruciating.

She couldn't keep going.

"Logan—"

He shook his head. "We need to keep moving."

She took a deep breath. "I don't think I can."

He turned and cupped her cheek. "You can. You will." His tone was unyielding.

"I won't make it far—"

"You will. I'll carry you, if I have to."

He was such a good, strong, and loyal man. She'd never met a man so real. With Logan, what you saw was what you got. He'd be there for you, no matter what. He wrapped an arm around her shoulders and pulled her to her feet.

They'd taken two steps when more bullets whizzed passed them, pinging off the stone walls.

"Keep going, Sydney." He set her against the wall. "Let me see where these guys are exactly."

He turned back, ducking his head around the stones. Sydney took a deep breath and edged along the wall, her side burning with each step.

She was passing a ruined doorway, when hands reached out and yanked her inside.

***

Bullets slammed into the ancient stones, flecks of

rock flying. Logan pulled back. Damn, he really wished he had his gun.

He turned back to Sydney, and his heart gave a hard thump. She was gone.

"Sydney!" A frantic whisper.

"Logan."

He heard her voice through a nearby doorway. He moved inside and saw she wasn't alone.

Drew Granger stood beside her.

Hearing Silk Road advancing, he nodded to the man. "I'm Logan. We need to get out of here. She's hurt and these guys are out to kill."

Drew nodded. "I know a way out. There's another exit out of the city."

Logan saw blood on the man's shirt. "You hurt?"

Sydney's brother swiped at his side. "It's nothing. I fell and cut myself."

Seeing no other choice, they followed him. Logan slipped an arm around Sydney again. He took as much of her weight as he could, and followed Drew as Sydney's brother picked a winding path through the ruins.

"There's another narrow exit through the outer walls." Drew's gaze dropped to Sydney's bloody shirt. A concerned look flowed over his boyish face. "Sydney, I'm sorry—"

"Not now." She reached out and squeezed her brother's hand.

Logan knew he had to get her out. That imperative was beating in his head. He needed to treat her wound and get her to safety.

They turned a corner, and Logan found the

barrel of a gun in his face.

"Fuck." Logan stared at Declan. "Where the hell have you been?"

"Stopped for a steak and a beer. You guys okay?" Then he saw Sydney's shirt and his gaze shot to Logan's.

The grim look in his friend's gray eyes made Logan's gut tighten.

"The treasure—" Drew began.

"Fuck the treasure," Logan bit out. "Your sister's life is far more important."

Drew paled and nodded.

"Drew, I'm Declan. We're here to get you out of here." Dec pulled out his secondary weapon and handed the gun to Logan. "Now, let's get moving."

Hale and Morgan moved past them, giving them cover fire. Logan was practically dragging Sydney now, as they moved through the ruins.

Then a Silk Road man stepped out of nowhere. He raised a weapon... Morgan spun, fired, and took the man down with a single shot.

But shouts echoed from all around them. More were coming.

"Move," Dec called out.

"Too many," Morgan shouted.

Now Logan saw them coming in from all directions. They'd received back up. He counted at least eight of them.

God, they weren't going to make it.

"Stop!" Piero's shout echoed across the ruins.

Logan looked over his shoulder and saw Piero advancing, surrounded by a large group of men.

Morgan was still on one knee, firing back.

"Logan."

He heard the desolation in Sydney's voice. She knew the situation was dire.

"Leave me. I'm slowing you down."

A muscle in his jaw ticked. "Never."

Her hands clenched on his chest. "Logan, I love you."

"Tell me later."

"Stop being stubborn. We might not have later."

"We will," he growled.

The Silk Road team closed in.

She squeezed her eyes closed and Logan gripped Sydney harder.

A high-pitched scream ricocheted around them. Logan's head snapped around. One of the Silk Road men fell back clutching his chest.

Another scream, and another man fell, a hand pressed to his neck. This time Logan saw a small dart sticking out of the man's skin.

Logan's gut went tight. *What the hell?*

***

Sydney leaned heavily against Logan, fighting back the pain.

With disbelief, she stared at the group of people creeping up behind the Silk Road men.

They wore modern clothes, but had white paint smeared across their cheeks and feathered headdresses on their dark hair. They were carrying spears and clubs.

More Silk Road thugs fell.

Logan pulled Sydney closer and Drew stepped nearer to them. Declan and the others moved in front of them, forming a protective wall.

Sydney didn't tell Logan that she could still feel blood pumping out of her wound.

Everything went still and quiet. All of the Silk Road members were down. She had no idea if they were unconscious or dead.

One of the warriors stepped forward. He had a strong face and a muscled body. His gaze drifted over them, studying them intently, his expression impassive. He had dark hair like most of his other warriors, but Sydney noted that his eyes were a bright green.

Something moved behind him, and she saw the jaguar stalk closer, brushing past the warrior's legs before it stopped to sit nearby.

The warrior spoke to them in what Sydney guessed was some local dialect. She looked up at Logan and he shrugged.

Drew pulled a small smartphone out of his pocket. He tapped on the screen and an electronic voice sounded from the phone.

"The treasure of my ancestors has been protected for centuries. It is not for the benefit of the greedy."

Drew swallowed and spoke slowly and clearly. "We come to study, to learn, to help you safeguard it." The translation sounded back in the local dialect.

The warrior tilted his head, studying Drew.

"Others have coveted it. Others have lied to get what they wanted."

Sydney straightened. "Then keep it hidden, if you want. Where it helps no one." Her words translated. She held up her bloody hand. "I've bled for your treasure, and right now, I just want to go home." She looked up at Logan, then back to the warrior. "You can keep your treasure. I found something far more valuable than gold and silver."

"And what is that?" the warrior demanded.

"I found myself, and I found love."

Logan's hand tightened on hers. "Sydney, I'm...I'm falling..."

"Come on, Logan," Dec said. "It's not that hard."

"What is it with you guys?" Morgan muttered. "Your timing always sucks."

"Let me do this myself," Logan growled at them. "Sydney, I'm falling in love with you, too."

"Logan." Her chest felt like it was going to burst.

Then her legs gave out.

"Sydney!" He scooped her into his arms.

Next thing she knew, he was laying her down.

"I need help here," he called out.

She was vaguely aware of his words translating on Drew's smartphone, and the warriors stoically watching.

Declan knelt beside her, tearing open a backpack and yanking out the first aid kit. He probed her wound, frowning, and she squeezed Logan's hand to stop from crying out.

"We need to get the bullet out. Logan, have a look in the kit and give her something for the pain."

Logan fished around in the kit and pulled out a pressure injector. He pressed it against her arm. "This'll help."

She found herself flickering in and out of consciousness. Her vision was blurring. She stared up at Logan's face, trying to hold out against the pain tearing through her like fire. "Logan."

"I'm here, Syd. Hang in there. Do you hear me?"

But the black blotches in front of her eyes were growing...and then there was nothing.

***

No. No. Logan clutched Sydney's limp hand. "Dec! Save her. Please."

Declan was working feverishly, Morgan kneeling beside him to help. He was using long tweezers and digging into the wound on Sydney's side.

Even with the pain relief and out cold, she reared up against the agony.

"Logan, hold her down."

He pressed his hands down on her shoulders, feeling her fight against him. Every pained sound she made cut into him.

It took far longer than Logan wanted, but finally, Dec pulled out the tweezers. On the end, was the bullet.

But there was blood everywhere.

"Pressure," Dec said. "Let's get the bleeding stopped."

Morgan pulled out a wad of gauze and pressed it over Sydney's wound. Logan took over, pressing down hard.

Logan looked up at the warriors still standing over them, weapons at the ready. "My woman is hurt. I need to get her to help. I don't care about your treasure, either. Just her." Only her.

The lead warrior watched him for a moment, then his gaze moved to Sydney.

Declan sat back, Sydney's blood staining his hands. "That's as stable as I can get her." He let out a deep breath. "Logan, I don't know if she'll make it. She's lost a lot of blood, and she's still bleeding. It's a two-day trek back to civilization, and she needs medical help right now. Out here, infection will likely set in fast."

"Any good news?" Logan asked, his insides turning cold.

"No. I'm sorry. She's going to be in a lot of pain, and I don't have enough painkillers for a two-day hike."

No. The word echoed in Logan's head. He cupped her face in his hands. "She's tough." She had to make it.

"Her life is worth more than the treasure?"

The warrior's translated words broke through Logan's agony. He looked up. "To me, her life is worth everything."

The warrior stared at Logan, like he could see right through him. Then he nodded.

The crowd of warriors parted, and a young woman stepped forward. She had the same green eyes as the lead warrior, her dark hair falling down her back. She knelt by Sydney, and with gentle hands, lifted Sydney's shirt. Logan lifted the bandages off.

The young woman clucked at the wound. Then she reached into the small pack hanging from her side. She pulled out a small wooden pot. She lifted the lid and Logan watched as the woman scooped out some sort of pungent, natural paste. She leaned over Sydney.

Logan grabbed her wrist. Behind them, the warriors all lifted their weapons.

"Our shaman will help," the warrior said.

Logan waited a beat, then let go of the woman's wrist.

Calmly, she started rubbing the paste onto Sydney's side. Suddenly, he noticed Sydney stopped struggling and her body relaxed. Next, the woman pulled a small bottle containing brown liquid from her pack. She gestured for Logan to lift Sydney's head.

He did, and the woman poured some of the liquid into Sydney's mouth. A second later, Sydney sat bolt upright with a gasp.

"Logan?"

"Sydney. Take it easy. You're hurt."

"God, there's a burning in my throat. It tastes horrible." She blinked, her gaze focusing on the woman kneeling by her side.

"She put some sort of poultice on your wound, and she gave you some liquid medicine."

Sydney's brow knitted. Then she looked down and lifted her shirt.

Logan looked at her wound...and froze. *No way.*

He heard his friends gasp.

Before his very eyes, he saw Sydney's wound healing, the edges of her torn flesh knitting together.

How was this possible? Logan shook his head. He pulled Sydney closer and looked up at the warrior.

The man gave him an enigmatic smile. The shaman woman patted Sydney's arm, then rose gracefully, and went to stand by the warrior's side.

"Our treasure was never gold or silver—" the warrior said "—but the knowledge of the plants of our home and their healing bounty." Another warrior stepped forward, holding something in his hands. He held it out and Logan saw it was a knotted quipu. The man rested it on Logan's palms.

"I give that knowledge into your safekeeping." A serious smile. "Along with much of the gold and the silver of our treasure. As your woman said, it does no good hidden away."

Logan's hand tightened on the knotted string. "Why? Why give it to me?"

"When I look at you and your woman, I see the souls of warriors. Honest. Brave. True." He gave a single nod, as though the subject was closed.

Then the warrior called out something that Drew's translator couldn't decipher. The warriors all started to pull back.

"Wait," Logan said. "What about these men?"

"The cloud forest will take care of them. We will see to it."

The unconscious Silk Road members were flung

over shoulders. Then, the descendants of the Warriors of the Clouds disappeared quietly into the ruins.

Sydney stirred. "Wild Man? I'd really like it if you took me home."

He pressed a kiss to the top of her head. "My pleasure, Syd."

Chapter Thirteen

Morgan had decided she quite liked the cloud forest—even with the jaguars and black market mercenaries in it.

She pushed through some vines, following the others, and glanced at her watch. They should be getting close to Laguna de los Condores. She still felt pumped, energy buzzing through her. It was the same after every mission where they found the treasure and beat the bad guys. Best feeling in the world.

It was going to take some time to process that they'd not only found the ancient treasure of the Warriors of the Clouds, but also some miracle cure. Morgan still couldn't believe she'd seen Sydney's wound heal before her very eyes.

They'd just checked it again a few miles back. The skin was still a bit pink, but other than that, perfectly healed. Damned incredible.

Ahead, she watched Logan scoop a tired and protesting Sydney into his arms. After a short argument Morgan couldn't quite make out, Sydney finally settled her head against Logan's broad shoulder.

God, the looks on their faces. Morgan shook her head. She couldn't believe that in under a year Dec, Cal and now Logan had all tumbled down the steep, rocky cliff of love. And Logan—wild, grumpy Logan—now had love stamped all over his rugged features.

Maybe miracles did happen.

Nah, Morgan wasn't planning to drink the Kool-Aid. She'd tried numerous times, subdued her own nature and desires, to find a decent guy.

She was done. She had her work, her friends, and her trusty vibrator, Big Red. That was enough for her.

"Man, I feel like a pizza."

Morgan glanced at Hale and snorted. "I'll call for delivery. You're paying the tip, though."

He pulled a face at her, then his gaze moved to Logan. "Never picked the big buy to be the next one to topple."

"So, you signing up to be next on the list?"

A vaguely horrified look crossed Hale's handsome face. "What? No. Too many nice ladies out there. I think I should be kind and share myself around."

Morgan snorted. "I seem to recall Callum saying that, and look at him."

"Maybe *you'll* be next, Kincaid."

Her snort this time was rude.

Hale laughed. "Right. He'd have to be a brave man."

As Hale moved to catch up with Declan, Morgan acknowledged the sting of pain in her chest. *Screw that.* She deliberately turned her thoughts to Silk Road.

The bastards were really becoming a problem and something had to be done. She just wasn't sure what. How did you fight people who stayed in the shadows?

"Come on, Kincaid," Dec called back. "Catch up."

Morgan lengthened her stride and pushed all the tangled thoughts out of her head.

***

Logan leaned back on his large leather couch, picked up the remote, and flicked on his television.

The couch dipped as Sydney sat beside him. She looked all pressed and elegant in her slacks and silk shirt. She set two glasses and a plate of food on his coffee table.

On the TV, the news was on. "Today, the anonymous discoverer of the Andes Miracle Cure released the recipe to the public. It looks like no pharmaceutical company will be raking in the profits on this one. Clinical trials are only in the early phases, and the full extent of the mixture's healing properties is not yet known. But the potential appears to be limitless."

Sydney leaned her head on his shoulder. "Logan O'Connor. Hero."

He scowled at her. "Shut up."

She grabbed the long beer glass she now made him drink his beer from and handed it to him. Then she picked up her glass of wine. She took a sip and made a humming sound. Blood rushed to his cock. Damn, that was exactly the same sound she made when he was thrusting inside her.

And he tried to spend as much time as possible doing that. Those harrowing moments in the Andean forest, where he'd thought he was losing her, still haunted him. He needed to prove to himself daily that she was alive and his.

"I spoke to Drew."

Her words scattered the little fantasies he was concocting in his head. "How is he?"

She smiled. "The new CEO of Granger Industries is as happy as a pig in mud. I cannot believe that it was his dream job all along. There I was, suffering through the work, while he was secretly pining to run the company."

Well, at least the guy was staying out of trouble.

"He's also organizing a special exhibit of Cloud Warrior artifacts at the Smithsonian later in the year, in conjunction with the Peruvian government."

"Good." Logan liked to think that the warrior who'd gifted him the trust of taking care of the treasure would be pleased. "I love you." He pressed a kiss to her hair, pulling it out of the fancy twist. He was planning to mess her up a little.

She smiled up at him. "Logan, you didn't even hesitate that time. Or get that twitch under your eye—"

He sank his hands into her hair and tugged her back against him. "Shut it. I really do love you." So much it hurt sometimes. "And what do you have to say to me in return?"

Her smile widened. "I made you nachos."

He scowled at her. "That's not what I meant."

She sat up and grabbed the plate off the coffee table. She held it out to him. "No? How about I'm loving my new job at Treasure Hunter Security?"

She'd taken over the business and investment side of THS. Darcy was in joyous convulsions...she'd never loved dealing with that side of things, preferring to work on her computers. Meanwhile, Sydney was loving it.

Logan pinched her. "Tell me what I want to hear, woman."

She leaned down and sank her teeth into his bottom lip. "How about I'm grateful every day that I hired Treasure Hunter Security and ended up with a wild, stubborn alpha male by my side, on a crazy adventure into the Andean cloud forests?"

"Better." He twined his hand in her hair. "But that's not what I was after."

"Hey," she said. "Watch the nachos."

He looked down at the plate and then his eyes narrowed. "Did you put Camembert on my nachos?"

"I'm not using that stuff in the can, Logan. It's not cheese. Try this, you'll like it."

With a growl, he grabbed the plate and set it back on the coffee table. He tumbled her on top of him, lying back on the couch. His hands snuck under her shirt. "Tell me."

She snuggled into him. "I love you, Logan. All of you. Every wild inch of you."

Damn. There it was. He never got tired of

hearing her say that. He yanked her closer for a kiss. "And I love you, Sydney Granger. Completely. Every beautiful, sexy inch of you."

***

Sydney leaned forward, searching through the files in the drawer. Darcy was scary smart, but her filing system was a disaster. Sydney needed the originals of the investment documents she was working on.

She closed the cabinet drawer with a sigh, eying the rest of the cabinets filling the small filing room at the back of the Treasure Hunter Security warehouse. She'd already organized the electronic filing system, and it looked like she'd need to get someone in to sort out this mess as well.

Large hands circled her hips from behind, making her squeak. Sydney found herself spun around and pinned up against the exposed brick wall beside the filing cabinets by a big, muscled body.

"You know these sexy schoolmarm skirts drive me crazy." Logan's voice was a husky growl. He leaned in closer, his teeth scraping against her neck.

Instant desire. It had only been weeks since she'd tumbled head over heels in love with this big, wild man, but what she felt grew stronger and deeper every day.

His lips landed on hers, deepening into a kiss. She kissed him back, always hungry for him. She felt his hands slide down her leg, then grip the hem of her pencil skirt, lifting it up. Her breathing hitched.

"Yes," she murmured against his lips.

"Will you two quit making out." Darcy's shout from out in the main warehouse. "I know what you guys are doing in there."

Logan lifted his head and growled. Sydney stifled a laugh.

"We have company incoming," Darcy added. "Mom and Dad are back from their dig and on their way in."

Logan groaned and Sydney gasped. She pushed against his chest. She wasn't meeting the Wards all mussed up.

When Logan finally stepped back, Sydney got busy straightening her clothes. "Persephone Ward and Dr. Oliver Ward. Living legends." She fiddled with her hair.

Logan reached out and touched her cheek. "Nervous?"

"A little." She straightened her collar. "I know you're close to them."

"They've always treated me like family. And they'll love you." He leaned forward and gave her a quick kiss. "Like I do."

Sydney's chest warmed, like it did every time this man said those words to her, but she couldn't help but be nervous. For so long she'd lived in a place where she was judged on everything, and where she'd never quite fit and never quite found happiness.

Now she'd found a man who was hers, and a place where she felt she belonged. She wanted Declan, Callum, and Darcy's parents to like her.

As she and Logan stepped out of the filing room, she saw Declan and Layne appear from upstairs. Declan's hair looked a little mussed and Layne's cheeks were flushed. Sydney bit her lip. It looked like she and Logan weren't the only ones making out in dark corners.

Layne bounced on her feet. "I can't *wait* to hear about your parents' trip. Your dad's dig at Petra in Jordan sounds so fascinating."

"And of course, Mom discovered a hidden hoard of gold artifacts," Declan added dryly.

There was a roar of a motorcycle and through the front windows, Sydney saw a fast, sleek motorcycle pull up. The man set his booted feet on the ground and flicked the bike's stand down. The two riders took their helmets off.

Callum Ward and Dani Navarro were both as sleek as their transport. Callum looked a lot like Declan—dark and dangerous. Dani—a world-renowned photographer—laughed at her fiancé before he reached over and kissed her.

These two looked like the perfect match. Sydney glanced at Logan's big form beside her. No one would glance at them and think they were a perfect match. The wild, rugged former SEAL and the stylish, society-raised woman. Her gaze drifted down his arms, taking in his tattoos and muscles. Her belly quivered. She didn't care. They worked together, and they were perfect for each other.

Callum and Dani walked in. "Hi," Callum called out. "Mom and Dad are right behind us."

The history professor and the treasure hunter. Sydney clasped her hands together. The pair really did sound like chalk and cheese. A little like Logan and Sydney.

Logan dropped onto one of the tattered couches that filled part of the warehouse space. Before Sydney could say anything, he reached up and tugged her into his lap.

"Logan! They'll be here in a minute—"

"You keep looking at me like you were and I'll drag you back into the file room."

She struggled against him. "Don't mess up my—"

He reached up and tugged her hair out of its neat twist, the pale strands falling around her shoulders. She opened her mouth to give him a piece of her mind, but he silenced her with his lips, and kissed her. Hard.

She struggled for a second before she gave in and kissed him back, her hands sliding into his shaggy hair.

"So, this is the young lady who tamed our Logan."

The sharp female voice had Sydney scrambling off Logan's lap. As she stood, she took in the tiny woman staring at her. The woman's piercing gray gaze seem to be cataloguing everything. Sydney touched her hair and realized it was a mess. She saw Logan get to his feet beside her.

Dammit. She'd just been caught making

out...and not even in a dark corner.

"Logan, my boy." The woman moved forward, bustling with contained energy. He leaned down and the woman kissed his cheeks, then touched his hair. "You need a haircut."

He grunted.

The woman rolled her eyes. "I've known you long enough to know that means you'll ignore me." Her gaze run over his face. "You look..." she tilted her head "...happy."

Then Persephone Ward's gray gaze moved back to Sydney.

The older woman was short, but had a compact, fit body. Her hair was a lovely shade of ash-gray that went with the gray eyes she'd given to two of her children. Sydney found it hard to believe this tiny woman had given birth to three children, including two strapping, former Navy SEALs.

"So, you're Sydney."

"I am, Mrs. Ward. It's a pleasure to meet you."

The woman waved a hand. "Call me Persephone, please. Mrs. Ward makes me feel old."

"Heard you still have that magic touch for finding treasure," Logan said.

Persephone straightened and winked. "Of course I do." She looked at Sydney. "I heard you two discovered some treasure of your own in South America, including a magical healing cure."

"Yes," Sydney answered.

Now Persephone's gaze narrowed. "And you gave it away? Anonymously? No fame, no fortune?"

Sydney felt the woman censure. Startled,

Sydney glance at Logan and saw he was grinning. She looked back at Persephone. "Ahh..."

"Percy, leave them alone."

Sydney glanced over and saw a man, flanked by Declan and Callum, striding toward them. She blinked. He was...an older but still sexy version of his sons.

Oliver Ward blew every stereotype of a stuffy, older professor out of the water. He had a toned body, and his hair was threaded liberally with gray. *Oh, boy.* Layne and Dani only had to look at this man to know they were going to be very lucky ladies in the future, if Declan and Callum aged the same way as their father.

"Professor Ward," Sydney said.

He reached out and shook her hand, shooting her a charming smile. "Oliver, please."

Oh, boy. Oliver Ward was one hell of a silver fox.

"Quit dazzling the girl, Ward." Persephone slapped her husband's chest. "My husband has been making students and coeds speechless from the first day he stepped foot in a university."

"And I still only have eyes for you, my darling treasure hunter." He slipped an arm around his wife's shoulders.

She sniffed.

"Your Sydney is lovely, Logan," Oliver said.

Logan pulled Sydney tight against his side. "I know. I'm a lucky man."

"And I hear you've taken over the accounts and business side of THS from Darcy," Oliver added.

"I'm the lucky one around here," Darcy said with a grin.

Persephone gave a shudder of horror. "Let's not talk about business or accounts." Another shudder. "We've made reservations downtown at our favorite restaurant. Good food, good wine, good company. And time to discuss any upcoming expeditions."

Oliver Ward's face turned serious and he looked at his sons and daughter. "I think we also need to discuss one less pleasant topic...Silk Road."

Persephone scowled. "I dislike the fact that this group keep trying to kill my children."

"I'm not overly fond of that either, Mom," Declan said.

"And you'll have all my help with that," Sydney added. "They were after my brother and nearly killed us all. They have to be stopped."

Persephone smiled at Sydney. "I think I like you, Sydney." Then she clapped her hands. "But first, let's have some wine."

As everyone headed out to the parking lot, Sydney moved to grab her coat from behind the reception desk. Logan reached out and took it, helping her into it.

He turned her, cupping her cheek. "Darcy might think she's lucky that you've taken over some work from her, but I'm the lucky one. Having you here, in my bed every night, loving me."

"I love you every minute of every day, Wild Man."

He pressed a quick kiss to her lips before moving his mouth down along her jaw until he nipped her earlobe. "Let's eat fast and then head home," he murmured. "I'm not letting anyone get in the way of loving my woman."

"Quit making out, you guys," came Darcy's exasperated shout from the door. "Let's go."

Sydney leaned into Logan, where she belonged, and laughed.

I hope you enjoyed Logan and Sydney's story!

There are more Treasure Hunter Security adventures on the way! The series will continue with UNFATHOMED, Morgan's story, out in January 2017.

For more action-packed romance, read on for a preview of the first chapter of *Among Galactic Ruins,* the first book in my award-winning Phoenix Adventures series. This is action, adventure, romance and treasure hunting in space!

Don't miss out! For updates about new releases, action romance info, free books, and other fun stuff, sign up for my VIP mailing list and get your *free box set* containing three action-packed romances.

Visit here to get started:
www.annahackettbooks.com

FREE BOX SET DOWNLOAD

JOIN THE ACTION-PACKED ADVENTURE!

Formats: Kindle, ePub, PDF

Preview: Among Galactic Ruins

MORE ACTION ROMANCE?

**ACTION
ADVENTURE
TREASURE HUNTS
SEXY SCI-FI ROMANCE**

As the descending starship hit turbulence, Dr. Alexa Carter gasped, her stomach jumping.

But she didn't feel sick, she felt *exhilarated*.

She stared out the window at the sand dunes of the planet below. Zerzura. The legendary planet packed with danger, mystery and history.

She was *finally* here. All she could see was sand dune, after yellow sand dune, all the way off into the distance. The dual suns hung in the sky, big and full—one gold and one red—baking the ground below.

But there was more to Zerzura than that. She knew, from all her extensive history training as an astro-archeologist, that the planet was covered in ruins—some old and others beyond ancient. She knew every single one of the myths and legends.

She glanced down at her lap and clutched the Sync communicator she was holding. Right here she had her ticket to finding an ancient Terran treasure.

Lexa thumbed the screen. She'd found the slim, ancient vase in the museum archives and initially thought nothing of the lovely etchings of priestesses on the side of it.

Until she'd finished translating the obscure text.

She'd been gobsmacked when she realized the text gave her clues that not only formed a map, but also described what the treasure was at the end. A famed Fabergé egg.

Excitement zapped like electricity through her veins. After a career spent mostly in the Galactic Institute of Historical Preservation and on a few boring digs in the central systems, she was now the curator of the Darend Museum on Zeta Volantis—a private and well-funded museum that was mostly just a place for her wealthy patron, Marius Darend, to house his extensive, private collection of invaluable artifacts from around the galaxy.

But like most in the galaxy, he had a special obsession with old Earth artifacts. When she'd gone to him with the map and proposal to go on a treasure hunt to Zerzura to recover it, he'd been more than happy to fund it.

So here she was, Dr. Alexa Carter, on a treasure hunt.

Her father, of course, had almost had a coronary when she'd told her parents she'd be gone for several weeks. That familiar hard feeling invaded her belly. Baron Carter did not like his only daughter working, let alone being an astro-archeologist, and he *really* didn't like her going to a planet like Zerzura. He'd ranted about wild chases and wastes of time, and predicted her failure.

She straightened in her seat. She'd been ignoring her father's disapproval for years. When she had the egg in her hands, then he'd have to swallow his words.

Someone leaned over her, a broad shoulder brushing hers. "Strap in, Princess, we're about to land."

Lexa's excitement deflated a little. There was just one fly in her med gel.

Unfortunately, Marius had insisted she bring along the museum's new head of security. She didn't know much about Damon Malik, but she knew she didn't like him. The rumor among the museum staff was that he had a super-secret military background.

She looked at him now, all long, and lean and dark. He had hair as black as her own, but skin far darker. She couldn't see him in the military. His manner was too...well, she wasn't sure what, exactly, but he certainly didn't seem the type to happily take orders.

No, he preferred to be the one giving them.

He shot her a small smile, but it didn't reach his dark eyes. Those midnight-blue eyes were always...intense. Piercing. Like he was assessing everything, calculating. She found it unsettling.

"I'm already strapped in, Mr. Malik." She tugged on her harness and raised a brow.

"Just checking. I'm here to make sure you don't get hurt on this little escapade."

"Escapade?" She bit her tongue and counted to ten. "We have a map leading to the location of a very valuable artifact. That's hardly an escapade."

"Whatever helps you sleep at night, Princess." He shot a glance at the window and the unforgiving desert below. "This is a foolish risk for some silly egg."

She huffed out a breath. Infuriating man. "Why get a job at a museum if you think artifacts are silly?"

He leaned back in his seat. "Because I needed a change. One where no one tried to kill me."

Kill him? She narrowed her eyes and wondered again just what the hell he'd done before he'd arrived at the Darend.

A chime sounded and the pilot's voice filtered into the plush cabin of Marius' starship. "Landing at Kharga spaceport in three minutes. Hang on, ladies and gentlemen."

Excitement filled Lexa's belly. Ignoring the man beside her, she looked out the window again.

The town of Kharga was visible now. They flew directly over it, and she marveled at the primitive look and the rough architecture. The buildings were made of stone—some simple squares, others with domed roofs, and some a haphazard sprawl of both. In the dirt-lined streets, ragged beasts were led by robed locals, and battered desert speeders flew in every direction, hovering off the ground.

It wasn't advanced and yes, it was rough and dangerous. So very different to the marble-lined floors and grandeur of the Darend Museum or the Institute's huge, imposing museums and research centers. And it was the complete opposite of the luxury she'd grown up with in the central systems.

She barely resisted bouncing in her seat like a child. She couldn't *wait* to get down there. She wasn't stupid, she knew there were risks, but could hold her own and she knew when to ask for help.

The ship touched down, a cloud of dust puffing past the window. Lexa ripped her harness off, trying—and failing—to contain her excitement.

"Wait." Damon grabbed her arm and pulled her back from the opening door. "I'll go first."

As he moved forward, she pulled a face at his broad back. *Arrogant know-it-all.*

The door opened with a quiet hiss. She watched him stop at the top of the three steps that had extended from the starship. He scanned the spaceport...well, spaceport was a generous word for it. Lexa wasn't sure the sandy ground, beaten-up starships lined up beside them, and the battered buildings covered with black streaks—were those laser scorch marks?—warranted the term spaceport, but it was what it was.

Damon checked the laser pistols holstered at his

lean hips then nodded. "All right." He headed down the steps.

Lexa tugged on the white shirt tucked into her fitted khaki pants. Mr. Dark and Brooding might be dressed in all black, but she'd finally pulled her rarely used expedition clothes out of her closet for the trip. She couldn't wait to get them dirty. She tucked her Sync into her small backpack, swung the bag over her shoulder and headed down the stairs.

"Our contact is supposed to meet us here." She looked around but didn't see anyone paying them much attention. A rough-looking freighter crew lounged near a starfreighter that didn't even look like it could make it off the ground. A couple of robed humanoids argued with three smaller-statured reptilians. "He's a local treasure hunter called Brocken Phoenix."

Damon grunted. "Looks like he's late. I suggest we head to the central market and ask around."

"Okay." She was eager to see more of Kharga and soak it all in.

"Stay close to me."

Did he have to use that autocratic tone all the time? She tossed him a salute.

Something moved through his dark eyes before he shook his head and started off down the dusty street.

As they neared the market, the crowds thickened. The noise increased as well. People had set up makeshift stalls, tables, and tents and were selling...well, just about everything.

There was a hawker calling out the features of his droids. Lexa raised a brow. The array available was interesting—from stocky maintenance droids to life-like syndroids made to look like humans. Other sellers were offering clothes, food, weapons, collectibles, even dragon bones.

Then she saw the cages.

She gasped. "Slavers."

Damon looked over and his face hardened. "Yeah."

The first cage held men. All tall and well-built. Laborers. The second held women. Anger shot through her. "It can't be legal."

"We're a long way from the central systems, Princess. You'll find lots of stuff here on Zerzura that isn't legal."

"We have to—"

He raised a lazy brow. "Do something? Unless you've got a whole bunch of e-creds I don't know about or an army in your back pocket, there isn't much we can do."

Her stomach turned over and she looked away. He might be right, but did he have to be so cold about it?

"Look." He pointed deeper into the market at a dusty, domed building with a glowing neon sign above the door. "That bar is where I hear the treasure hunters gather."

She wondered how he'd heard anything about the place when they'd only been dirtside a few minutes. But she followed him toward the bar, casting one last glance at the slaves.

As they neared the building, a body flew outward through the arched doorway. The man hit the dirt, groaning. He tried to stand before flopping face first back into the sand.

Even from where they stood, Lexa smelled the liquor fumes wafting off him. Nothing smooth and sweet like what was available back on Zeta Volantis. No, this smelled like homebrewed rotgut.

Damon stepped over the man with barely a glance. At the bar entrance, he paused. "I think you should stay out here. It'll be safer. I'll find out what I can about Phoenix and be right back."

She wanted to argue, but right then, two huge giants slammed out of the bar, wrestling each other. One was an enormous man, almost seven feet tall, with some aquatic heritage. He had pale-blue skin, large, wide-set eyes and tiny gills on the side of his neck. His opponent was human with a mass of dreadlocked brown hair, who stood almost as tall and broad.

The human slammed a giant fist into the aquatic's face, shouting in a language Lexa's lingual implant didn't recognize. That's when Lexa realized the dreadlocked man was actually a woman.

A security droid floated out of the bar. Its laser weapons swiveled to aim at the fighting pair. "You are no longer welcome at the Desert Dragon. Please vacate the premises."

Grumbling, the fighters pulled apart, then shuffled off down the street.

Lexa swallowed. "Fine. I'll stay out here."

"Stay close," Damon warned.

She tossed him another mock salute and when he scowled, she felt a savage sense of satisfaction. Then he turned and ducked inside.

She turned back to study the street. One building down, she saw a stall holder standing behind a table covered in what looked like small artifacts. Lexa's heart thumped. She had to take a look.

"All original. Found here on Zerzura." The older man spread his arms out over his wares. "Very, very old." His eyes glowed in his ageless face topped by salt-and-pepper hair. "Very valuable."

"May I?" Lexa indicated a small, weathered statue.

The man nodded. "But you break, you buy."

Lexa studied the small figurine. It was supposed to resemble a Terran fertility statue—a woman with generous hips and breasts. She tested the weight of it before she sniffed and set it down. "It's not a very good fake. I'd say you create a wire mesh frame, set it in a mold, then pour a synthetic plas in. You finish it off by spraying it with some sort of rock texture."

The man's mouth slid into a frown.

Lexa studied the other items. Jewelry, small boxes and inscribed stones. She fingered a necklace. It was by no means old but it was pretty.

Then she spotted it.

A small, red egg, covered in gold-metalwork and resting on a little stand.

She picked it up, cradling its slight weight. The

craftwork was terrible but there was no doubt it was a replica of a Fabergé egg.

"What is this?" she asked the man.

He shrugged. "Lots of myths about the Orphic Priestesses around here. They lived over a thousand years ago and the egg was their symbol."

Lexa stroked the egg.

The man's keen eyes narrowed in on her. "It's a pretty piece. Said to be made in the image of the priestesses' most valuable treasure, the Goddess Egg. It was covered in Terran rubies and gold."

A basic history. Lexa knew from her research that the Goddess Egg had been brought to Zerzura by Terran colonists escaping the Terran war and had been made by a famed jeweler on Earth named Fabergé. Unfortunately, most of its history had been lost.

Someone bumped into Lexa from behind. She ignored it, shifting closer to the table.

Then a hard hand clamped down on her elbow and jerked her backward. The little red egg fell into the sand.

Lexa expected the cranky stall owner to squawk about the egg and demand payment. Instead, he scampered backward with wide eyes and turned away.

Lexa's accoster jerked her around.

"Hey," she exclaimed.

Then she looked up. Way up.

The man was part-reptilian, with iridescent scales covering his enormous frame. He stood somewhere over six and a half feet with a tough face that looked squashed.

"Let me go." She slapped at his hand. *Idiot.*

He was startled for a second and did release her. Then he scowled, which turned his face from frightening to terrifying. "Give me your e-creds." He grabbed her arm, large fingers biting into her flesh, and shook her. "I want everything transferred to my account."

Lexa raised a brow. "Or what?"

With his other hand, he withdrew a knife the length of her forearm. "Or I use this."

Also by Anna Hackett

Treasure Hunter Security
Undiscovered
Uncharted
Unexplored

Hell Squad
Marcus
Cruz
Gabe
Reed
Roth
Noah
Shaw
Holmes
Niko
Finn

The Anomaly Series
Time Thief
Mind Raider
Soul Stealer
Salvation
Anomaly Series Box Set

The Phoenix Adventures
Among Galactic Ruins
At Star's End
In the Devil's Nebula
On a Rogue Planet

Beneath a Trojan Moon
Beyond Galaxy's Edge
On a Cyborg Planet
Return to Dark Earth
On a Barbarian World
Lost in Barbarian Space

Perma Series
Winter Fusion

The WindKeepers Series
Wind Kissed, Fire Bound
Taken by the South Wind
Tempting the West Wind
Defying the North Wind
Claiming the East Wind

Standalone Titles
Savage Dragon
Hunter's Surrender
One Night with the Wolf

Anthologies
A Galactic Holiday
Moonlight (UK only)
Vampire Hunter (UK only)
Awakening the Dragon (UK Only)

For more information visit AnnaHackettBooks.com

About the Author

I'm a USA Today bestselling author and I'm passionate about *action romance*. I love stories that combine the thrill of falling in love with the excitement of action, danger and adventure. I'm a sucker for that moment when the team is walking in slow motion, shoulder-to-shoulder heading off into battle.

I write about people overcoming unbeatable odds and achieving seemingly impossible goals. I like to believe it's possible for all of us to do the same.

My books are mixture of action, adventure and sexy romance and they're recommended for anyone who enjoys fast-paced stories where the boy wins the girl at the end (or sometimes the girl wins the boy!)

For release dates, action romance info, free books, and other fun stuff, sign up for the latest news here:

Website: AnnaHackettBooks.com

Printed in Great Britain
by Amazon

86291852R00113